BLANKETY BLANK

A MEMOIR OF VULGARIA

D. Harlan Wilson

Published by Raw Dog Screaming Press
Hyattsville, MD

First Paperback Edition

Cover image: Brandon Duncan
Book design: Jennifer Barnes

Printed in the United States of America

ISBN 978-1-933293-57-8

Library of Congress Control Number: 2008922400

www.RawDogScreaming.com

Other Books by D. Harlan Wilson

Fiction Collections

The Kafka Effekt

Stranger on the Loose

Pseudo-City

Novels

Dr. Identity, or, Farewell to Plaquedemia

Criticism

*Technologized Desire: Selfhood & the Body
in Postcapitalist Science Fiction*

"The Egg Man"
lyrics by
The Egg Men

Egg Man!
Egg Man!
Egg Man!
There's an Egg Man in an Egg House committing Egg Raids on Mojo!
Apocalypse of petroleum sunsets
in a garbage can
and a blender full of green margaritas.

Sitting on a tuffet in the sky, the Egg Man goes
"Flimflam! Flimflam! I am the Egg Man!"
But then the clouds move in and the Egg Man throws
himself onto the wasteland (yeah yeah baby yeah).

Egg Man!
Egg Man!
Egg Man!
There's an Egg Man in an Egg Dojo kung fu fighting against a Stick Man!
The Egg Man wins.
The Egg Man wins.

Slouching towards the rough beasts, the Egg Man goes
"Flimflam! Flimflam! I am the Egg Man!"
Or does the Egg Man go "The world will decompose
in the depths of a frying pan" (yeah yeah baby yeah yeah)?

Egg Man!
Egg Man!
Egg Man!
There's an Egg Man in an Egg Kitchen making a mushroom omelet!
He runs out of olive oil
and all that's left
is blankety blankety blank. Fuck it!

Standing in a Styrofoam igloo, the Egg Man goes
"Flimflam! Flimflam! I am the Egg Man!"
And when the dawn cracks open, the Egg Man knows
it's time to scram (yeah yeah baby yeah yeah yeah).

DISCLAIMER

This is a memoir, which is to say, a collection of my personal thoughts, feelings and experiences, which is to say, a work of absolute truth, which is to say, a work of unadulterated fiction, which is to say, a wild extrapolation of people, places and things that may or may not exist in the real world, as in a novel, or a movie, or the news, or history, or a dream, or, as it were, a memoir...

DEDICATION

For me!

Table of Contents

The Silo

"A little to the left now. To the left. That's not left!"

The construction workers looked down at Mr. Van Trout. They nodded and gave him reassuring salutes.

"Don't patronize me! Just do your damned job!" He stormed into the garage, picked up a hammer and pounded nails into random objects—into the wall, into the construction table, into a basketball (it exploded), into a ski, into a freezer door, into the hood of his Mercedes...into his hand.

A tsunamic curse resounded across the landscape of McMansions.

His wife opened a door and poked out her head. "What was that noise?"

Mr. Van Trout glared at her. "I pounded a damned nail into my hand. See?" He showed her. She covered her mouth. He marched out of the garage, slamming the door on his wife's face as he passed. He thrust the maimed hand into the blue sky. Blood coursed down a blond-haired forearm.

"You did this!" he shouted at the construction workers. But he forgave them immediately. They had managed to place the domed roofing of the silo in precisely the right spot, and now a swarm of mop men polished its aluminum exterior with big chamois, gently in some areas, furiously in others. Soon the roof shined like an aged celebrity's grin. The shine blinded one construction worker. He slipped, fell, and parachuted to the grass. Mr. Van Trout put on sunglasses and admired the man's descent.

The crane operator rolled down the window and leaned his elbow out. "Got a tetanus shot lately? My little girl died of a tetanus shot. Rusty syringe."

Mr. Van Trout clicked his tongue. He studied his hand and went inside the house.

9

His wife's nose was bleeding. She held her head over the kitchen sink and allowed the blood to leak into the drain, clutching her long, silver-streaked hair in a pony tail behind her. "I don't think you broke it," she said calmly. "But I'm going to let it coagulate on its own."

Mr. Van Trout yanked the nail out of his hand and put it into the silverware basket of the dishwasher. "I'm sorry," he said, wrapping the hand in paper towels. He went downstairs to the basement.

Moans of pleasure. A laugh. Some grunting, squealing...Layke was watching porn. Soft porn, her father detected—no genital interaction or close-ups. She sat cross-legged on the floor in front of a wall-screen.

"At least go to the bathroom," grumbled Mr. Van Trout.

Layke winked at her father. "Cable's out in the bathroom." She cocked her head. "What's your deal?"

"No deal." Clutching the wad of blood-soaked paper towels, he proceeded into the laundry room. He turned on the cold faucet of an industrial sink, unwrapped the towels, and held his hand under the water. It felt good. He squirted liquid soap into the hole. It stung. He tried to stick his finger in the hole and clean it out, but even his pinky was too thick. He found some Q-tips and used one of those. Then he held his hand under the water until it went numb.

He turned off the sink. The hole continued to bleed, although not as badly. He could see through his hand. He could see through it into the sink's drain. There was a piece of cauliflower down there. Or a big tooth. He couldn't tell.

Now what? Did people get stitches when they nailed holes into their hands? Or did their hands take care of the holes themselves? When was the last time he had a tetanus shot? Five years ago? Fifteen years ago? How often were people supposed to get tetanus shots nowadays? As often as you were supposed to get them five years ago? As often as you were supposed to get them fifteen years ago? Is the number of years for five years and fifteen years the same? If so, what is that number of years? If not, how many numbers of years fall between the former and the latter? And which number is correct, despite contemporary medical opinions? Despite old-fashioned medical opinions? To what degree does the effect of a tetanus shot vary depending upon one's physiology and genetic disposition? Was Mr. Van Trout going to die? Was he ready to die? Then what? Heaven? Did he believe in Heaven? Did he believe in God? What about Jesus? Was he Jesus? Would the hole in his hand be mistaken for stigmata? Do stigmata exist? Should he nail a hole into his other hand and tell people he had stigmata? Why would he do that? Why would he do anything? What would people think if he walked around with only one hole in his hand? That he was only a partial incarnation of Christ? That he was posing as a partial incarnation of Christ? That he had a birth defect? That he accidentally nailed a hole into his hand in a fit of irrational anger?

Mr. Van Trout blinked.

He soaked up the blood with a warm washcloth, squeezed a dollop of Neosporin into the hole, put band-aids on the openings, and bandaged his hand in gauze. Then he went back upstairs to check on the status of the silo.

———

A Short History of the Silo

The first documented appearance of the silo occurred in ancient Greece circa 20,000 B.C. in the middle of what is known as the Mesolithic or Middle Stone Age. While it had no apparent use-value other than being a tall, hollow edifice into which one might enter and walk around in circles, the silo's popularity quickly gained momentum. Soon every functional, financially capable socialite had built a silo alongside his home, and although a silo intermittently served as a locale for the odd novelty party or card game, the structures remained outside the boundaries of practicality and utilitarianism. This lasted for millennia. Circa 7,500 B.C., the silos, which by now spanned the length and breadth of the country like so many shotgun shells on a checkerboard, began to entertain a religious significance. They did not serve as churches or sanctuaries, but as idols to be worshipped. The specific reason for this turn of events is unknown, albeit many critics believe it had to do with a cataclysmic event (among the most popular suspects are an alien invasion, the awakening of a race of hibernating dinosaurs, a turbo-charged ice age involving various "NASCAR glaciers," and a two week downpour of acid rain). The idolization of the silo on a communal level was an ephemeral phenomenon. Not half a century later, most of them were being employed as outhouses, garbage bins and, in select townships, private barber shops. They continued in this vein for approximately 89 centuries, past the birth of Christ, into the dark ages and beyond, until, in the fifteenth century, documented evidence of a silo being used as a farming storage unit appeared in "The Tail's Tale," a fabliau ostracized from Geoffrey Chaucer's *The Canterbury Tales* by Edward III because of its allegedly overclever subject matter and lyricism. In the story, an armadillo mistakenly eats an undead shrew that invokes sentience in the armadillo's tail. The tail turns against its owner. Capable of ventriloquism, it throws its voice into various inanimate objects, daring the armadillo to stand on its hind legs, calling its manhood into question, and ultimately aspiring to drive it insane. The plan works. The armadillo comes to believe that it is a masochistic vampire and sucks itself dry, underscoring the moral of the story:

Know what you are before you eat of it.

The silo played no significant role in "The Tail's Tale." It was mentioned only peripherally.

Pure in heart, the farmer passed a silo,
filled with corn as yellow as the devil's eyes...[1]

But finally the silo had a true purpose, one that realized the structure's full potential and endured to the present day.

There were exceptions to the contemporary rule. Sometimes people filled their silos with flower petals, for instance. Sometimes they filled them with coffee beans, or eucalyptus leaves, or Super Balls. Typically aromatic items.

---

1 Translated from Middle English by Stanley Ashenbach.

———

Mr. Van Trout thought: The world is bleeding from every orifice. And the world has too many orifices...Or is it orifi? He had difficulty remembering which words deserved an *i* or an *es* in their plural forms. He was sure about porpoise: the plural was porpoises. He was sure about fungus: the plural was fungi. But what about orifice? Was the plural orifices or orifi? Both forms seemed incorrect.

In the kitchen, Mrs. Van Trout continued to lean over the sink. Her nose had stopped bleeding. A thin, fragile stalactite of blood hung from the bridge of her nostrils, and she kept her head steady, stiff, trying not to break it.

Mr. Van Trout reached out to put a hand on her shoulder. She stopped him with a back kick aimed at the groin. The kick didn't connect, but her husband got the picture.

"I said I was sorry."

A pause. Then, in the faintest whisper: "I know you did. It's not about apologies. You'll break it. You'll break it if you touch me."

"It's gotta break at some point."

"Not on my watch."

Mr. Van Trout chewed the insides of his cheeks. "Your daughter's downstairs masturbating again." He exited the kitchen.

———

Outside the construction workers had finished the job. They stood at attention in front of the silo in an organized line. They were clean, well-groomed, tanned, and looked like Ken dolls except for their potbellies: spit-shined yellow hardhats, bright white grins, designer plaid shirts and jeans, and construction boots. A few of the more fashionable workers had on cowboy boots.

The foreman stepped out of rank and approached Mr. Van Trout. Cast in the shadow of the silo, the two figures looked like generals walking across a battlefield to meet and discuss terms. Mr. Van Trout seemed confused by the formality, especially when the foreman began to clash two orchestra cymbals together and high step as if in a marching band. Apparently this was some kind of promotional technique; in any case, the construction company was reputed throughout the neighborhood for its musical appetite. Mr. Van Trout ignored the foreman. The silo was up. The silo looked good. That's all that mattered.

The foreman continued to play the cymbals after the two men reached handshaking distance and came to a halt. Mr. Van Trout waited patiently for him to stop, wincing each time the cymbals collided. His patience threaded into anger. He could be polite when he wanted to, but it was much easier to be a bastard. He stomped on the foreman's toe. The foreman wore steel-toed boots and it didn't hurt. He took the cue, however, and threw the cymbals over his shoulders. They hit the grass and quietly rolled into the street.

Gongs rang in Mr. Van Trout's ears. "The silo looks good!" he screamed.

"You're screaming," the foreman told him.

"I wonder why!"

"You did it again."

"Did what!"

"Screamed."

"Screamed!"

"You did it again."

"Did what!"

"Screamed."

"Screamed!"

"You did it again."

Mr. Van Trout tightened his lips. He cleared his throat a few times. He waited…"The silo looks good," he said in a normal voice.

The foreman glanced over his shoulder. He made a surprised face, as if he had never seen the silo before. "I think you'll find it to your liking, sir. Care to test the unit out?"

Mr. Van Trout shook the foreman's hand and walked towards the silo. The rank of construction workers opened and he passed through them and stepped onto an ironclad ladder that zigzagged up the silo like a fire escape. Some of his neighbors had gathered in the street. Shielding their eyes, they craned back their necks and examined the great height of the silo as their children busied themselves in driveways with magnifying glasses, burning anthills and vagabond beetles. A few children used miniature blowtorches.

At nearly 200 feet, the silo was by far the tallest structure in the neighborhood, seconded only by an egregious turret affixed to the left flank of the Onderdonk's McMansion at the top of the street. A little walkway with a hand railing circled its top. Mr. Van Trout climbed the ladder and passed through a trap door in the walkway. Panting, he closed and locked the door, then leaned against the railing. The heat of the sun kissed his bald spot. The air smelled like a man-made lake, clean and pure with just the slightest hint of toxicity. It was cooler up here by at least a few degrees. No breeze, though.

Mr. Van Trout took deep, calculated breaths. The climb up the ladder was the most exercise he had done in awhile. He wasn't necessarily out of shape. He took walks. Sometimes he did curls. But he wasn't in shape either. Not like he used to be. Not even close.

A bead of sweat dripped from his ear lobe. Mr. Van Trout removed his shirt. A modest roll of fat fell over his belt. He threw the shirt off of the walkway. He laid his chest and arms and cheek onto the smooth, warm surface of the silo's crown.

More neighbors gathered below, all of them wives or Mr. Moms and their kids. Children outnumbered adults now. There were hundreds of them. From the sky it looked like the street was on fire, flames humming and crackling over the din of insect screams.

Neighbors & Pain

Troy's parents named his sister Sheba. They also gave the name to the family dog, a German shepherd who attacked Rutger Jr. at its leisure. Once Sheba gave Rutger Jr. rabies. Immediately after being bitten, the smooth trapezoid of skin that separated the boy's eyebrows into two distinct entities sprouted a tuft of hair. The result? A menacing unibrow.

In addition to rabies, Rutger Jr. was treated and immunized for lycanthropy, his pediatrician having some experience in that area.

———

A Short History of the Werewolf

The existence of werewolves dates back to the earliest forms of intelligent civilization. In the Indo-European tradition, werewolves derive from berserkers, Nordic warriors who dressed in bear or wolf hides and were notorious for their ferocity on the battlefield. Off the battlefield berserkers had an equally legendary reputation for their horn-sharpening, drag racing and bocce ball skills. No matter what space they inhabited, however, they always kept their hides on, even when they bathed and fornicated. It is rumored that this persistence in remaining clothed at all times—what nowadays might be called gymnophobia (fear of being naked)—led to the (un)natural grafting of animal skin onto human flesh. Eventually berserkers insisted that their women do likewise, and at birth, they sewed cub pelts onto their children's flesh like jumpsuits. Thereafter berserkers began to slide out of their mother's wombs with cub pelts intact. Being a werewolf, or at any rate being furry, became the normative state of berserker existence, if only retroactively, as the term "werewolf" didn't itself exist until years later.

Early werewolves of this fraternity evolved fangs in much the same way as they did exteriors: by means of self-production. For millennia, berserkers filed their teeth to sharp points for use in battle until one day they were born with sharp teeth. Not so with tails. From the beginning, tails were artificial extensions of the berserker body, a body that never welcomed and adopted the extension as its own. Any hypothetical or actual descendents of berserkers that exist today would thus be expected to possess fake tails or, more likely, none at all, insofar as tails, considering their limited utilitarian value, have always served for the purposes of fashion, and in some cases social status, within lycanthropic communities.

Berserkers are one among many originary instances of lycanthropy, all of which have their own ways, means and idiosyncrasies. Virtually no other werewolf myth, for example, sees the element of transformation span over the course of millennia; that is, it took thousands and thousands of years for berserkers to turn into werewolves, at which point they stayed werewolves, whereas in other myths, prone and/or infected parties transformed to and from werewolves in a matter of seconds, usually incited by some kind of nocturnal force (e.g. the proverbial full moon). In the vegetable depths of Guatemalan history, there are people who transform in accordance with their breathing: inhalations render them ferocious, hairy, saber-toothed beasts, and exhalations render them docile, smooth-skinned, smiling hombres, so that every moment of their lives is a moment of change, unless one elected to hold one's breath, which would maintain biological stasis for as long as the breath could be held in. In terms of transformative speed and dynamism, these *al trannies* (trans. *alquitrán des niños* or tar babies), as they were called, fell on the opposite side of the spectrum from berserkers. Between the two species lay the dimpled ocean of variation.

Certain characteristics of the werewolf condition are common to many demographic, geographic, temporal and cultural locales. These include allergies to silver, being the seventh son of a seventh son, being cursed by evil magicians, shapeshifting as an effect of a full moon, hypertrichosis, porphyria, and a fetish for German opera, among others. No symptom, however, spans all four categories. No symptom but one.

The unibrow.

Originally the presence of a unibrow on one's forehead signified witchery. Suspects were apprehended by the law and either beheaded, stoned, or burned at the stake, usually the latter.

Society viewed the unibrow as an insignia of demonic power and enchantment. Over time this perception changed. People began to attribute the facial feature to animal-related deeds. Those that possessed it were incriminated for acts such as chicken hawking, piggery, bestiality, and, in due course, shapeshifting.

While today the unibrow is no longer associated with lycanthropy, it continues to harbor negative connotations, designating somebody who is either dull-witted or untrustworthy. Gastroenterologists equate it with a lack of athleticism.

———

Rutger Jr. loved Sheba. She was skinny and had big guns.

He stared at her from a sandbox in the back yard. She and Marylou Fitzgerald ran through a sprinkler and slid across a wet banana and threw glasses of lemonade at each other. Then Marylou Fitzgerald took off the bottom of her swim suit. Her bush looked like a pinecone.

They saw him.

Sheba sicced Sheba on Rutger Jr. The boy ran into the front yard and tried to take refuge in the silo. Locked door. He outran Sheba eight circles around the silo before getting dizzy and tripping over his own feet.

The dog bit off his ear lobe.

"Daaad!"

Mr. Van Trout looked up from the pterodactylic wingspan of a newspaper. He pushed out his lips. Did somebody put the tea kettle on?

"Daaad!"

Setting aside the newspaper, he climbed out of his chair, walked to the front window and peered outside, sipping a highball.

Sheba had his son in a headlock. Rutger Jr. struggled helplessly in the dog's grasp as his bloody face turned purple and his eyes bulged out of his skull. Mr. Van Trout stared at the brawl in disbelief. Since when did dogs have biceps? He couldn't believe the size of Sheba's bicep. It looked like a bodybuilder's...

Mr. Van Trout retrieved a double-barrel from a gun closet and kicked open the front door. He marched into the yard and shot off two slugs.

Sheba yipped and leapt into the air as if bounced off of a trampoline. Rutger Jr. clutched his chest, coughed, gasped.

Mr. Van Trout eyeballed the dog. Shivering, the dog took two steps backwards. Mr. Van Trout tossed the gun into a bush and made for Sheba.

Sheba made for home.

Despite being slightly overweight, the Dutchman was quick and could run fast in short bursts. He caught up to the dog almost immediately and dropped an elbow on its back. The dog crumpled, howled. Mr. Van Trout picked it up by the tail, swung it around his body once, twice, three times...and released his grip.

Sheba flew into the Conklin's driveway and somersaulted into Troy, who had been watching. The dog assimilated Troy into its somersault. They picked up speed as they rolled into the garage and crashed into a stack of sporting goods.

Sheba (the girl) ran into the front yard. Marylou Fitzgerald followed, tugging on a pair of jeans. "You asshole!" exclaimed Sheba. The force of the exclamation caused one of her breasts to leap out of its casing. Mr. Van Trout felt dirtyoldmannish. He looked away.

Sheba covered her breast. "I'm telling my dad! Daaad!" She ran inside.

Marylou Fitzgerald mooned Mr. Van Trout and went home.

———

Troy wasn't a chronic bully. Occasionally he fell prey to bouts of friendliness and altruism. For the most part, though, he was a rotten apple, particularly when it came to Rutger Jr., who he picked on religiously. He hated something about the kid. The way he looked? The way he talked? The way he acted? He wasn't sure. But sometimes he sat in his basement and thought about it, never realizing that what he hated in Rutger Jr. was what he saw in himself.

Rutger Jr. looked plain. He had a plain haircut and a plain body and plain clothes and a plain personality. He spoke plainly, both in terms of directness and vocabulary, the latter of which was limited but not deficient.

Troy was almost as plain as Rutger Jr. except for an obnoxious set of snaggleteeth and one leg that was two inches shorter than the other. He had to wear a special shoe with a pump to even out his body. The shoe critically wounded his sense of selfhood and subjected him to considerable ridicule, but only by children that were bigger, tougher, and more psychologically scarred than him. This didn't include Rutger Jr., who, in spite of having a common body type, was comparatively weak, uncoordinated, and psychologically stable.

Troy's snaggleteeth exacerbated his insecurities. But his father wouldn't buy him braces, even though he had the money. It took a year of begging to get Mr. Conklin to buy him an orthopedic. He spent half of that year getting Mr. Conklin to acknowledge him as his son, a fact that he had denied since Troy could remember being able to form coherent sentences.

"You're an orphan. A complete stranger, really," his father reminded him on a regular basis.

Usually Troy slumped away. Once he said, "No I'm not. I have DNA evidence." He brandished a bouquet of papers. Mr. Conklin took them, uncrinkled them, read them.

"This doesn't prove anything."

Troy looked at his father expectantly.

Ronald Conklin removed his glasses and eyed the boy. "Where'd you get this?"

"Dr. Pachulski. Mom and I went to see him last week." A forensics expert, Dr. Pachulski lived three McMansions down the street.

Mr. Conklin threw the papers aside. "You and your mother. All you do is gang up on me." Troy hoped his father would spank him. Instead he ignored him. Troy slumped away. His father put his glasses back on. "The sun will come out tomorrow," he whispered.

————

The sound of crying eclipsed the sound of the summer breeze.

Troy staggered out of the garage, convulsing, fish hooks caught in his arm, a black eye. He cried like a kicked puppy. Sheba followed him. Limping and bleeding, the dog cried like a spanked child.

Sheba (the girl) blustered outside. She looked beat up. She cried and clawed at herself and ran around in crooked circles.

In the basement of her house, Mrs. Conklin cried into a pillow. She cried softly, but a muffled wail escaped from time to time. This was an everyday occurrence and unrelated to the matter at hand.

Rutger Jr. felt his ear. It was wet. He cried. He looked at his hand. Blood. He cried harder. He felt his ear again. It wasn't all there. He cried harder and harder as he scurried across the lawn on all fours looking for the bitten off lobe.

The summer breeze wafted across the skin of Rutger Sr.'s face.

————

He picked up his son and carried him inside. Blood poured out of his ear.

Francisco walked into the foyer sipping a cosmopolitan from an oversized martini glass. She dropped the glass. It shattered on the tile. "What happened!"

"Neighbors and pain," said Rutger Sr.

"Oh my God!"

Rutger Sr. rested Rutger Jr. on the floor. He had passed out from crying too hard. Rutger Sr. kept pressure on his ear and told his wife to do the same with a gauze pad until he got back.

Francisco panicked. "Where are you going? Don't leave!"

He left.

———

Statistic

The rise of bullying in the United States in the last two decades among children, regardless of class, race or gender, has prompted the Bureau of Justice to declare bullying an art form. As this art form is still in a larval stage, what dictates "good," "bad" and "nominal" bullying is subject to multiple interpretations. Classes in bully execution, defense and abstention are offered in some schools as early as the first grade. 76% of parents with children enrolled in public schools have condemned this development. The Bureau of Justice encourages parents to focus on the Big Picture, insisting that "bully pedagogy" will ultimately lead to a better quality of life and an unprecedented decrease in the use of pharmaceutical products by adults.

———

Ronald Conklin believed children should be seen, not heard, so once a day he put Sheba and Troy over his knee and spanked them, guilty as they were for making noises or speaking out loud. Sheba was twelve years old and he still spanked her. It hurt, but she didn't cry. She lay on his knee with the same blank expression worn by her father.

Mr. Conklin sold medical imaging equipment. He worked out of his home, confined to a subterranean office all day and night, emailing and phoning doctors and trying to bullshit them into buying monstrous hunks of machinery on rollers. Half the time he looked at porn. His family barely saw him. He often forgot he had a family, sometimes by accident, sometimes by choice.

On Sundays, Mr. Conklin converted his office into a wine cellar, swiveling one of its walls to reveal an impressive stock. He was reading a comic book and polishing off a bottle of 1996 Château Lafite Rothschild Pauillac when a knock came to the door. Startled, he spilled a drop of the wine onto his desk. He quickly licked it up and yelled, "WHAT!!!"

No response. He heard his wife weeping on the other side of the door.

He opened the door. "What."

She sniffled. She tried to say something, failed. Mr. Conklin waited.

Finally she said, "The children. Th-they're...They're crying."

"Children? What're those?"

Mrs. Conklin ran across the basement and threw herself on a couch.

Mr. Conklin shut the door. He poured another glass of wine, drank it in one enormous swallow, opened the office door, went upstairs, and opened the front door.

Rutger Van Trout marched up his driveway, snapping the fingers of a dishwashing glove onto his hand. Along the way he stepped on Troy, who rolled around as if on fire. Sheba (the girl) stood rigid and quiet as a statue at the sight of her father, thin rivulets of mascara describing her cheeks. Sheba (the dog) flailed on its back.

"What's the problem here?" said Ronald Conklin.

"Your kids, shithead," said Mr. Van Trout as he picked up the dog by the scruff, rammed his hand down its throat, fished around for a moment, and yanked out the gory contents of its belly. He tossed the dog aside. Mr. Conklin watched in confusion. Mr. Van Trout fingered through the gore until he found his son's ear lobe. He put it in his pocket and shook off the residual mucous. "One more time, Conklin. One more time, motherfucker! Then I'm coming after you." He pointed a dramatic finger at him.

Mr. Conklin shook his head. "Do I know you?"

———

Mr. Van Trout placed his hand on Rutger Jr.'s forehead. Rutger Jr. moaned. Nearby his ear lobe lay atop a glass of ice.

"Get me a razor. Get me some thread and a needle. Fill a syringe with anti-lycanthropic serum. Go!"

Mrs. Van Trout gasped. "Anti-what? He needs a doctor! We need to take him to the hospital!"

"Doctors are evil. Hospitals make people sick. Do as I say!"

"What's going on?" said Layke, standing at the top of the stairs. She had on a beige ballerina outfit. "Is Rutger all right?"

"Go to your room. Get some normal clothes on!"

"Rutger Van Trout!" screamed Francisco.

"Uitroep!" Mr. Van Trout went and got the supplies himself.

When he came back, his wife and daughter were dragging Rutger Jr. across the living room by his ankles. A skid mark of blood stained the floor.

"Stop!" shouted Mr. Van Trout.

"He needs a doctor!" shouted Mrs. Van Trout.

Layke did a *pas de bourrée*.

Mr. Van Trout ordered them to go into the kitchen. They didn't. He used THE VOICE: a low, basso, grumbling noise that dependably scared the shit out of them, or at least let them know Rutger Sr. was deadly serious (even though the true function of THE VOICE was supposed to be good-humored and sociable). They scurried away. Rutger Sr. petted Rutger Jr.'s forehead. His son was partly conscious. He injected him with a sedative followed by the anti-lycanthropic serum. He threaded a needle. He removed his ear lobe from the glass of ice and methodically sewed it back on. The last thing he did was shave the patch of skin between Rutger Jr.'s eyebrows.

"The sun will come out tomorrow," he whispered.

Costume Party

Mr. Van Trout thought: Life is essentially just a long sequence of increasingly intense assfucks that one tries and fails to avoid as one lumbers through the manure of daily existence. I can smell manure. Who's fertilizing their damned yard this time of year? I once dreamt that I was a yard. A great, flat body of Astroturf. All day long I stared at the sky. No clouds. Two planes and a flock of geese. A paraglider. Then somebody turned on the sprinklers, so I stood like a man and dove into the neighbor's swimming pool. It was full of cold green peas. I swam laps—back and forth between the sidestroke and freestyle. Did I have that dream last summer? It might have been when I was eight years old. That was a fine age. I started growing nose hairs. Everybody made fun of me for being a late bloomer and having to wear air purifiers in my nostrils. I remember when I took the filters out for three days. My head filled with dust and I had to bang it against the blackboard like an eraser to keep it clean. I always liked to keep clean. But one can't be clean without getting dirty. In the absence of pollution, hygiene wouldn't exist...

"Hors d'oeuvre, sir?" A platter of miniature piglets tightly wrapped in bacon slices squirmed and squealed on the silver platter, trying to break their bonds. Mr. Van Trout frowned at the appetizers. He looked up and frowned at the waitress.

Her face was a porcelain dinner plate with raw eggs for eyes, a splash of cocktail sauce for a nose, a stick of asparagus for a mouth. The eggs slowly slid down the kidney-shaped plate. She looked like a two-dimensional Down syndrome patient.

"Are you all right?" asked Mr. Van Trout. He had on a blond gorilla suit.

"Sir?" The buds of the asparagus convulsed as she spoke.

He panned down. Decent body. Big cans. Wide hips. So-so legs with chiseled calves. Long smiles in her black, second-rate hose.

A pig squealed in agony.

"No thank you."

She walked away.

———

Mrs. Francisco Van Trout believed in skeletons. Not the kind that people hid or stowed away in closets, but the kind that lived beneath the flesh. She believed skeletons had a mind of their own, a mind separate from the bodies they fortified. Her skeleton had a mind of its own, for instance. Sometimes it did things she didn't tell it to do. She suspected it was haunted.

"By what?" asked Mrs. Bert, who wore a suit of black Spandex. Painted onto the front of the suit was a white skeleton.

"By a skeleton," replied Mrs. Van Trout.

"Whose?"

"Voltaire's, I think. Maybe Jimmy Carter's."

"Jimmy Carter is still alive. Cryogenically anyway."

"That doesn't mean his skeleton is alive."

Mrs. Bert chewed her underlip. "Can we turn off the lights?"

Shrugging, Mrs. Van Trout removed a lawn dart from her purse and hurled it across the room. It struck the light switch. The room darkened. People screamed.

Mrs. Bert's skeleton glowed in the dark. But which one? The one that lived on the inside or the outside of her?

Mrs. Van Trout massaged her scalp, wondering about the condition of the skull that lay just a millimeter or two beneath the surface.

———

Dr. Pachulski tapped Dr. Tenbrook on the shoulder. Dr. Tenbrook looked over his shoulder. "Yes?" he said softly.

"Hey Mark."

"Good evening."

Dr. Tenbrook's costume was an exaggerated version of himself. Exaggerated mustache, exaggerated chin, exaggerated shoulders, exaggerated bulge in his groin. Dr. Pachulski told him the outfit was interesting.

"Interesting?"

Dr. Pachulski wasn't wearing a costume. "I'm not wearing a costume," he said.

"I can see that."

"Do you want to know why?"

Dr. Tenbrook fingered his chin. "Have you seen my wife?"

Dr. Pachulski fingered his chin. "Your wife? You're married? When did this happen?"

"It happened."

He decided to change the subject. "How's the chiropractor business?"

"Bone manipulator."

"Excuse me?"

"I prefer bone manipulator, not chiropractor. It's more direct." He grabbed Dr. Pachulski and cracked his neck. Dr. Pachulski collapsed. "See what I mean?"

———

A pubescent girl streaked through the costume party in her birthday suit. Punch sprayed out of one man's nostrils. Another man choked on a Vienna sausage. Layke spied on the streaker through two holes cut into the eyes of a life-sized Gerald R. Ford painting on the wall. The ex-president had on a Boy Scout uniform with shorts and knee socks.

———

"Mae West used to wear false nipples made out of pancake batter. True story.

And in the last film she made, *Sextette*, she wore nipples the size of full-grown pancakes. I'm not sure how they stayed intact. Are pancakes naturally adhesive? Maybe. *Sextette* came out in 1978. Who knows what kind of pancakes they had back then? Mae West died at 87. She wasn't buried in a coffin. They dug a hole, threw her corpse inside, filled the hole with pancake batter and waited for it to solidify. It didn't take long. True story. Some brands of pancake batter are like fucking cement, I'm telling you. In some smaller cities they're starting to make sidewalks out of pancake batter. In larger cities, too. Atlanta, for instance. There's a block made out of pancakes—sidewalks, streets, buildings, even fire hydrants and lampposts and traffic lights. They say no restaurants serve breakfast on that block. Who would? Buy yourself a bottle of maple syrup and you're all set. Then again, that assumes everybody eats pancakes for breakfast. I don't eat pancakes for breakfast. I eat eggs. I eat ham and grits. I'm a man. True story."

———

The soundtrack for *Breakin' 2: Electric Boogaloo* interrupted the arrangement of smooth jazz that emanated from the stained glass horn of the Van Trout's retro-futuristic Victrola compact disc player. A few partygoers began to disco dance. Others executed rudimentary breakdance moves—airplanes and airswipes, windmills and poplocks, bodyflares and downrocks—and one partygoer did a sequence of applejacks, dropping backwards onto all fours, kicking a leg high into the air, springing back onto both legs and then repeating the maneuver. A circle formed around the dancer and people began to plunge in and out of the mix.

Rutger Jr. lay in bed with his arms folded behind his head. He could feel the bass from downstairs thumping in his guts. He felt it in his ear lobe, too, which had healed, more or less, but it was still a little tender. A rerun of Fantasy Island played on the ceiling-screen. He turned up the volume.

He felt badly for Tattoo. Nobody really picked on him, not even Mr. Roarke, although every now and then he dealt the midget a belittling glance. But Tattoo was a slave. And he always looked sad. Even when he smiled. Knowing the actor who played Tattoo, Hervé Villechaize, committed suicide in the name of his sadness intensified the empathy Rutger Jr. felt for him. He said a prayer for the actor. "Feel better, Hervé," he prayed.

———

"Who puts a silo in their front yard?" said Jane Smith, huffing. Her costume was a glittery Venetian stick mask with a peacock feather.

"Who names her kid Jane when her last name is Smith?" said Sarah Winnowitz. Her costume was also a stick mask, although a much cheaper one, and it didn't have a feather.

"My husband's name is Smith!" Jane barked.

Gusty Erwin's costume consisted of a fake wart on her nose. She said, "Your maiden name is Smith, too."

Jane tightened her lips. "Bitch." She dropped her mask and glanced around the room. "Who has costume parties anyway? I mean, a costume party? Get real."

"Ladies," intoned Rutger Sr., appearing out of nowhere in love handle-friendly wrestling briefs and shiny knee-high boots. He resembled wrestling legend Bobby "The Brain" Heenan in his prime, complete with blond butt-cut and dimpled chin. He changed costumes once every fifteen minutes or so. "Are you enjoying yourselves?"

Happy faces snapped onto Gusty and Sarah. They said it was the best party the neighborhood had ever seen. Jane maintained a tart expression. Rutger Sr.'s chest hair was irregularly patterned and made her uncomfortable.

Hiking his briefs above his navel, Rutger Sr. gestured out a bay window with his chin and said, "She's a crossbreed. Stitched together from different materials. Wood and concrete staves, steel panels, cast concrete and iron, slabs of porcelain. I bought them at the hardware store! Right up there at Kingsland on 28th Street. Don't get me wrong. I didn't build the thing. I can't take credit for building the thing. But I challenge you to find me a better-looking, better quality unit than that son of bitch out there in my front yard. Can you do it?" He exhaled noisily, marveling at the vertical prowess of the silo.

———

Mr. and Mrs. Conklin crashed the party around eleven o'clock. They had disguised themselves as the Blainmeters with meticulous latex masks and pastel sweater vests. The Blainmeters were a gay couple who lived on Candlewood Drive. The Conklins-as-Blainmeters claimed the costumes that they intended to wear had been eaten by the dog. "Not to worry," said Mrs. Van Trout, taking their coats. "Dressing up is optional. But you're already here." She pointed across the room at the real Blainmeters. They hadn't worn costumes either. Seeing the impersonators, they waved and gave them two thumbs up.

Embarrassed, the Conklins retrieved their coats and ran home.

———

"Rutger's an asshole," said Mrs. Bert to Mrs. MacVengeance. She took a sip of punch. "I'd screw him, though. I'd screw anything. I'm a whore. Don't tell anybody, though. Ok?"

Mrs. MacVengeance said, "Of course not," then leaned to one side and not-too-furtively whispered the gossip into Mz. Veneklausen's ear. It spread across the room like an electric charge.

Mrs. Bert felt breathing on her neck. She turned. She yelped.

Rutger pulled his Tucan bill to one side. "You think I'm an asshole?"

———

A cockroach walked to the edge of a china cabinet on its hind legs...and died.

———

"Did you know cockroaches can walk on their hind legs before they die? True story."

"I don't think so."

"I swear. It's like a death throe or something."

"Death throe? How is that a death throe?"

"I'm not sure. I couldn't say for sure."

They observed one another.

"How many legs do cockroaches have?"

"Eight? At least six. Anyway they can stand on their hind legs and walk around like people, swinging their other legs like arms. Insectologists say it's a death throe."

"Entomologists."

"What's that?"

"Nothing."

They observed one another.

"Insects can't stand on their hind legs, dumbass, let alone walk around on them."

"Uh, yes they can."

"Uh, no."

"Well, cockroaches can."

"No."

"Dragonflies can."

"Dragonflies? No."

"Walking sticks can. They can stand right up there."

"Nope."

"Hmm. Well, that's all the insects I know."

"That's all the insects you know? There's a few more."

"I guess. I always get confused, though. Like with spiders. I can never tell the difference between a spider and an insect. Is a spider an insect?"

"No. It's a spider."

They observed one another.

"Goddamn these costume parties," said Trent Vandermuelen, taking off his fish head. "Everybody wants to have a costume party nowadays. What happened to the days when people would just hang out and get fucked up on gin martinis?"

Herman Underlay took off his sheep head. "There was a time when you didn't even have to preface the word *martini* with *gin*. It was understood. Then vodka came along. A vodka martini! Blasphemy."

From opposite ends of the room, both men's wives yelled at them to put their heads back on. They reluctantly obeyed, swallowing three shots of Southern Comfort apiece first.

They could barely hear each other through their heads. "Baa," said Mr. Underlay.

Mr. Vandermuelen said, "Why the fuck did Van Trout put a silo in his front yard? What is he fucking crazy or something? Crazy motherfucker."

"Baa," said Mr. Underlay.

Harry Bombgarten spiked the punch with a pint of Everclear, making little effort to be surreptitious, or rather, his effort to be surreptitious was so pronounced as to draw attention to the act of insurrection. Mr. Van Trout had taken a seat atop an armoire to keep an eye on the partygoers and make sure nobody stole anything. He spotted Harry straightaway, hopped off the armoire, and pushed his way through the crowd towards the would-be troublemaker, nodding and smiling and patting people on the shoulders as he went.

Sporting oversized sunglasses, a fedora, bear trap jaws and trench coat, Harry poured in the Everclear a dollop at a time. Mr. Van Trout folded his arms behind his back and stared at him.

"Just a dash of salt. Just a dash of salt," said Harry.

"There's already alcohol in there," said Mr. Van Trout.

Harry removed his sunglasses and scowled at the punch. "There's never enough alcohol in there."

———

Eliot Trinity Coots a.k.a. ETC a.k.a. Etcetera knocked on the window. Rutger Jr. got off the bed and opened it. Etcetera crawled in. He had a big sack with him. He opened it and dumped out five shrunken heads.

"Cool!" Rutger Jr. exclaimed.

"You like those?" Etcetera said. "My dad got 'em in Singapore. I think they're real. I think they belonged to people my dad mighta killed on a safari."

Rutger Jr. picked up a head and studied it like a math equation.

———

Unable to sustain the brunt of further conversation, the men broke out portable roulette tables and poker chips and dice and stacks of cards and BINGO stubs and exploded into a gambling frenzy. The frenzy was quickly put to sleep by the women, who disciplined the men at the top of their lungs, but not before a sizeable chunk of change traded hands.

———

Mr. and Mrs. Conklin crashed the party again around quarter to midnight. They had disguised themselves as the Estradas with meticulous latex masks, a stone-washed Mexican tuxedo for Ronald, and an Ecuadorian blouse for Madge. The Estradas were a Hispanic couple who lived on the west side of Cascade. The Conklins-as-Estradas claimed the costumes that they intended to wear had been ground up in the garbage disposal. "Not to worry," said Mrs. Van Trout, taking their coats. "Dressing up is optional. But you're already here." She pointed across the room at the real Estradas. They hadn't worn costumes either. Supervised by Mr. Van Trout, who was now wearing a striped

35

referee uniform, they wailed on a piñata with two-by-fours.

Annoyed, the Conklins retrieved their coats and stomped home.

———

Mr. Van Trout went to his office and unwrapped the bandage from his hand... He closed the hand. Quickly he opened it and stuffed cotton balls in the hole. Then he did another shot of Jäegermeister, rebandaged the hand, and returned to the party.

———

Troy Conklin aimed a BB gun at one of the Van Trout's windows, and fired...He missed. The BB hit the house and bounced back and hit Troy in the Adam's apple. He gasped for breath. He clutched his neck. His Adam's apple had disappeared. Had it shattered? Had he swallowed it? Terrified, he ran into the kitchen and quickly ate an apple, core and all, to replace the loss.

Meanwhile Marylou Fitzgerald and Sheba Conklin touched themselves while talking about boys over the phone.

———

Hors d'oeuvres grew cold...Hors d'oeuvres grew cold...

———

Layke took the *y* out of her name and laid it on her bed. She realized that *y*s were basically upside-down penises and wondered why her parents had put one in the middle of her name. Then she realized that all letters looked like penises if you perceived them from the right angle and wondered why her parents had given her a name full of penises. Then she put her *y* back.

_____

Dr. Tenbrook didn't speak to his wife on the walk home. She didn't know he operated under the alias of a superhero named The Gamehater, but he thought she should treat him like a superhero anyway, if for nothing else than he had his Ph.D. But she treated him like shit. She treated their goldfish better than him.

"I'm the Gamehater," he often said under his breath. His wife rarely heard him. If she did, she told him that mumbling was for infants and retards.

The Gamehater was well-known in the neighborhood. He had solved over ten crimes in the past year. None of the crimes had been acknowledged by the Law, since they weren't technically crimes at all (for instance, the time he busted Danny Winnowitz for having a bad hairdo, which turned out to be a simple case of adolescent bed head). He owned several costumes. His favorite was a skintight polyester getup covered in images of burnt Scrabble letters and Monopoly cards. As for superpowers, he possessed the ability to generate and disperse mentally destructive hate waves, a birth defect that had only manifested once, by accident, in junior high school. Caused by a random, seemingly insignificant act of bullying, the hate wave exploded across the campus of Forest Hills Central Middle School, momentarily lobotomizing or infantilizing students, teachers, janitors and administrators. Since then, he had never conjured another hate wave. But he never forgot the incident. And he was always on the lookout for history to repeat itself.

The Gamehater wasn't the only superhero in the GRIM (Grand Rapids Internal McSubübermensch). Many men and women had appropriated friendly neighborhood alter-egos to varying degrees of awkwardness and social misfitry. Few compared to the awkwardness and misfitry of The Gamehater, however, especially when he took action.

As Dr. Tenbrook and his wife shuffled up imitation marble stairs to their front door, he heard a scream. He looked at his wife.

"What's wrong?"

"Nothing. Excuse me." He turned and hurried down the stairs.

"Where are you going?"

"To the garage. To the back yard. To Indiana. What do you care?"

"Redneck." She went inside and deadbolted the door behind her.

Dr. Tenbrook paused in the driveway. He wasn't entirely sure what direction the scream had come from. He had been meaning to upgrade his alter-ego with audio implants, but it was difficult for him to spend money on things that he didn't really need. Maybe he hadn't heard anything.

He closed his eyes and contracted his eardrums.

Another scream. He darted into the back yard and disappeared into a row of ersatz palm trees.

The Royerson's McMansion was a mirror image of Dr. Tenbrook's except for a discrepancy in the color of its vinyl siding. The siding on his house was vaguely darker. Therefore it was vaguely superior. According to Dr. Tenbrook's logic, darker colors indicated a greater degree of power and charisma in the people who owned and exhibited the colors. Still, the sidings were pretty similar. The McMansions had to be closely examined to tell their colors apart, and there was no telling in the nighttime. But knowing the difference between them was enough. One night last year, Dr. Tenbrook (à la the Gamehater) snuck onto the Royerson's property and painted the house lemon yellow. By morning, however, the house had reverted to its original color. He accounted for the anomaly in one of four ways: 1) Mr. Royerson had seen him and hired a crew of moonlight painters to restore the color of the house the moment Dr. Tenbrook finished vandalizing it; 2) he had dreamt that he vandalized it; 3) the house possessed a self-cleaning device that constantly maintained its primary color; 4) he was partially color blind and painted the house its original lemon yellow color. He doubted the latter possibility more than the others. In any case, the experience had taught him to broaden his perspective. He never confessed the (potential) crime to Mr. Royerson. No reason to hatch a chicken that's already been counted, he told himself.

After some confusion, Dr. Tenbrook determined that the screams were not coming from the Royerson's McMansion, but from a large gopher hole in the

Astroturf. The back yard was a Par 3 and the hole lay just short of the green. Dr. Tenbrook took off his suit. He yanked open his shirt. Buttons popped off and exposed the insignia of his present costume, a Clue board with a no smoking strike through it.

The Gamehater dipped his head into the gopher hole.

A small gaslight illuminated the underground chamber. Cast on the wall were the silhouettes of two naked teenagers, one boy, one girl, facing each other, arms at their sides, the tips of their noses almost touching. Every ten seconds one of the teenagers opened its mouth and screamed. They took turns. The Gamehater didn't know them. He didn't know their silhouettes anyway.

"Psst," he said.

Slowly the teenagers turned their heads. He could see the whites of their eyes.

"Everything all right down here?" he said.

Silence.

"Everything all right down here? I said is everything all right down here?"

"I'm being raped," said one of the teenagers in a grave, subhuman voice.

The Gamehater stared at them.

"I'm being raped," said the other teenager in a shrill, choked-chicken voice.

The Gamehater puckered his lips.

Above ground robotic fireflies glimmered, synthetic crickets chirped, and a flaming airplane tore across the starry sky.

"Good evening." The Gamehater pulled out his head. He dropped a business card in the hole, just in case the teenagers decided they needed his help, and on his way home, he reminded himself not to hate the players, but to hate the game.

———

"Check this out."

Sig Zeeland rolled up his sleeve and flexed his bicep. He was a professional bodybuilder. The bicep inflated like one of Dizzy Gillespie's cheeks and sprouted a cloak of purple veins.

"Hey!" Resenting the hungry-for-attention character of her husband, Frieda Zeeland rushed across the living room, tore off her shirt and snapped into a Front Double Biceps pose, nudging the middleweight Sig out of the way with her heavyweight hip. Her hunger for attention was far greater than his, and she made sure that every crease, every bulge, every cut in her bronze upper body operated at full capacity.

Partygoers watched idly as the couple nudged one another with greater force. A few people passed out. It was getting late.

———

Mr. Van Trout thought: Where's Lou?

Lou Diamond Phillips moved in down the street three years ago. He owned the biggest McMansion on the block. He lived alone, flying to L.A. whenever he had to make a film, which wasn't that often since he struck the ninety-year-old mark. He didn't come to the costume party despite being sent a homemade invitation and RSVPing in the affirmative. Sipping an MGD Light, the actor read through a manuscript for *La Bamba IV: Ritchie Goes Zombie (Again)*. Periodically he glanced at the TV.

———

"The remembered past is always more attractive in the retrospective present than it is in the actual past. It's true what they say: memories are superior to experience."

"Who says that?"

"*They* do."

———

Mr. and Mrs. Conklin crashed the party again around 1:30 a.m. They had disguised themselves as the Novaks with meticulous latex masks and fat suits.

The Novaks were an obese couple who lived in Ohio. The Conklins-as-Novaks claimed the costumes that they intended to wear had been struck by lightning. "Not to worry," said Mrs. Van Trout, taking their coats. "Dressing up is optional. But we don't know you."

"We're from Ohio," said Mr. Conklin-as-Mr. Novak.

"Oh."

The Conklins-as-Novaks looked around the house. All the guests had left. In the living room, Rutger Sr. and Layke guffawed as they battled with pugil sticks and tumbled into piles of garbage. Rutger Jr. ate piñata candy and watched a silent film on a wall-screen.

Saddened, the Conklins retrieved their coats and slouched home.

Bmw Futique

The car was only six months old and only had 860 miles on it and the owner only wanted $95,500 for it.

"Horseshit."

———

Confucian Analect

The superior man spins the wheel of fortune and realizes that ignorance is the nightmare of consciousness. And when the wheel stops turning, he peels off his skin and sells it for the price of eight beans.

———

He put aside the newspaper, picked up the phone, and dialed the owner's number. He set the speaker tone for Camouflage 6. Deep, rumbling and computerized, his voice sounded like it belonged to a kidnapper calling for ransom money.

"Hello?"

"What's your problem?"

"What?"

"Fuck's your problem?"

The line went dead. He redialed.

"Hello?"

"Why'd you hang up on me?"

"You swore."

"Swore? Are you kidding me?"

"Who is this?"

"You know my name."

"Uhm...are you calling about the car?"

"Where do you get off selling a car like that? You've got a nerve, you son of a bitch."

The line went dead. He redialed.

"Hello?"

"Knock it off. Is the car for sale or what?"

"Pardon me?"

"The car. The BMW Futique. The one you advertised in the paper. The damned car. Are you selling it?"

"Who is this?"

He squeezed the neck of the phone.

"I'm calling the police."

"Lighten up. I'm only interested in the car. I want to know why you're selling it."

"I don't want it. That's why."

"You don't want it? That's your answer?"

"That's my answer. Do you want to look at the car or not?"

"I'll be over in two minutes."

"Wait—"

He hung up. "I'm going on a drive," he said. Nobody was in the room.

He put on a jacket and hat, found his keys, slid behind the steering wheel of a battered Mercedes Clydesdale II, pulled out of his driveway, and drove four miles across the Vulgaria of Quiggle Estates. He weaved in and out of children playing in the street. He dodged children who were hurled at his car by their parents.

He parked halfway on the Bert's front lawn. He hopped out of the Clydesdale and jogged to the front door. He knocked on it, took a step backwards, and folded his arms across his chest.

"Who is it?" said a tentative voice.

"Rutger Van Trout Senior."

The door opened. "Oh. Hi Rutger."

"Right. Where's the car?"

"Car?"

Rutger stared at him.

Aukland Bert said, "I'm confused."

Rutger rolled his eyes. "Do we have to go through this again? I just wanna give it a once over."

Pause. "Was that you on the phone?"

Rutger sighed. He tilted back his head and thrust his hands into his pockets.

"What's wrong with you?" asked Aukland.

Another sigh. "Nothing. Bye." He turned to leave.

Aukland licked his lips. "Wait. Come in. Come in."

Rutger went in.

————

Aphorism

An effective neighbor never licks his lips before tackling the job of being an effective neighbor.

————

Delorean-style 4-door w/snub-nosed front bumper. Rotary hybrid system. Heat-reflected glass. Projector beam lens bi-xenon headlights. 11 liter V24 engine w/flux capacitor. Fxns. as stick shift, automatic or voice-activated. Stainless steel acrylic lacquer clearcoat exterior. Hand-stitched burgundy leather interior. Scandinavian designer speedometer. Bang & Olufson holoviz on the dash w/sensurroundsound entertainment system. Sun roof w/telepathic open/close connection. Powered by fossil fuel, methane gas or corn husks. Heated door locks and seats. Knight Rider KITT brain w/roving Cylon redeye. Rocket thrusters. Quadruple exhaust. 5.0 googlebyte computer. Organic tires w/capacity to inflate to monster truck size. Multiframe body construction w/ capacity to transform into motorcycle and SUV (upgrade chip required). Top speed: 260 mph. 0-60 mph in 3.8 seconds. Detachable whale fin spoiler...

"Jeez," said Aukland. His son had sidled up next to him. Jeez was a miniature version of his dad: square and blond and muppetlike. "Where'd you come from?"

"A womb. Hi Mr. Van Trout."

Rutger dealt the boy a quick smile, then turned to his father. "I'll give you fifteen thousand for this piece of shit."

Aukland winced. "Rutger."

"Sorry. Hunk of junk."

"Piece of shit," Jeez echoed. Aukland asked him to go inside and play with his brother, Jeez II. Jeez stood there. His dad flicked him in the temple. Jeez ran inside bawling for his mother.

"Look what you've done, Rutger," Aukland said. "My son's in agony."

Rutger nodded. "So. Fifteen thousand. Do we have a deal?"

"Deal? Are you insane? This thing's brand new."

"Brand new my ass. Why are you selling it? You just bought it. Why'd you buy it? To sell it? That doesn't make sense. That thing started depreciating in value the second you drove it off the lot. Now you're selling it. That's dumb. D-U-M." As always, Rutger spoke in a tone that bewildered listeners. One could rarely tell if he was serious or kidding. Sometimes Rutger couldn't even tell.

Aukland said, "That's my business. I don't have to explain why I do what I do."

"I'm leaving. You're an idiot." He started to walk out of the garage. He stopped at the door. "Gimme the keys."

"Sorry?"

"The keys. To the car. Give'm to me."

"Yeah, right," Aukland smirked.

Rutger picked up a lead pipe and threatened to bash in the BMW's rear windshield. Aukland threatened to call the police again. Rutger tossed the pipe aside and said, "You think you can sell this car without telling a buyer why you're selling it? You think you can sell this car without letting a buyer test drive it? Do we live in the same universe? Are you a cartoon or a real person?"

Aukland furrowed his brow, considering the question. "I'm not a cartoon," he murmured.

"Gimme those damned keys."

———

Nothing appeared to be wrong with the car. Rutger drove it at top speed through the Vulgaria, the GRIM, and then out to Grand Haven. He cruised around looking at old refinished Victorians. He went to Spring Lake, rented a wet bike, vroomed through no wake zones, heckled water skiers, and sprayed sunbathers on anchored boats. Afterwards he tanned on the beach. A few hours later he returned to Quiggle Estates.

Aukland waited for him at the main entrance gate. His eyes were bloodshot and his hair was a campfire. In each hand he held a clump of weeds. "Rutger Van Trout!" he roared.

Rutger waved at him as he drove by.

———

Fifteen minutes later, in Aukland's driveway...

Rutger stepped out of the car and shut the door. He stretched.

He ducked.

A clump of weeds struck the driver's side window. Rutger inspected the window to make sure it wasn't scratched, then faced Aukland.

"Ok. I'll give you twenty thousand for this white trash sled."

———

Aukland hyperventilated and blacked out. He dreamt of an ancient Ferris wheel going 46 rpm. It came off of its hinges and rolled down the street. The wheel transformed into a flying saucer that leapt into the sky and began to destroy Quiggle Estates with a heat ray. It continued to rotate at a velocity of 46 rpm.

———

Description of the First Ferris Wheel

Invented by George Washington Gale Ferris Jr., the first Ferris wheel was built for the 1893 World's Columbian Exposition in Chicago. It weighed over 2,000 tons, stood more than 250 feet tall, and had the capacity to carry 2,160 people at the same time, supporting 36 gondolas the size of school buses. Cost of admission was 50 cents per revolution, each of which took 20 minutes. The Ferris wheel was intended to rival the grandeur of the Eiffel tower, the main attraction of the 1889 Paris Exhibition, albeit the former only stood a quarter of the latter's height.

———

On Flying Saucers

In *Flying Saucers: A Modern Myth of Things Seen in the Skies*, C. G. Jung argues that the predominance of post-WW2 UFO sightings is the result of a collective hallucination induced by, among other possibilities, a fervent desire to visualize round objects in the sky. UFOs, in other words, are archetypal images whose "simple, round form portrays the archetype of the self, which as we know from experience plays the chief role in uniting apparently irreconcilable opposites and is therefore best suited to compensate the split-mindedness of our age" (21). At the time of *Flying Saucers'* composition and original German publication in the 1950s, the threat of nuclear warfare and increasing overpopulation weighed heavily on Jung's psyche; he suspected that our "technological fantasies" were merely compensatory, a means of coming to terms with a world that was growing too small and unnatural for the specter of humanity. In a supplemental interview to the book, Jung is asked if flying saucers, notwithstanding their circular shapes, are inherently connected to Ferris wheels in some way. "They are one and the same," said Jung, "save certain key mystical incongruities."

———

Was he frowning before he awoke? Or did he awake and then frown? He didn't know. A dark circle had swallowed his face. It smelled like duck shit.

"Wake up!!!"

Thunder rang in Aukland's ears. He cried out.

Rutger tossed aside the megaphone, stuffed a sock in Aukland's mouth and helped him to his feet. "Are you going to make that noise again?"

Aukland's eyes bulged. He snorted and choked. Rutger yanked out the sock. Aukland doubled over, gasping, retching.

Rutger sighed. "Didn't you used to be a marine? Ten hut, for Chrissakes."

———

After an hour of intense haggling, Aukland gave up and sold the Futique to Rutger for $64,800, $30,700 below the blue book price of the car. It was a big loss, but only a scratch on the skin of his bank account, and he took pride in the fact that he never told Rutger why he was selling the car, despite Rutger's vehement psychological and verbal attacks on his character.

"I'll be back later to get my Clydesdale," said Rutger as he slid into the driver's seat of his new car. "Say hi to the wife for me."

———

He told the vehicle to turn on. Music sandblasted him from every direction. He said, "Stop," and checked the playlist. The Egg Men's "The Egg Man" was the only song Aukland Bert had programmed into the music box. He told the car to play the chorus.

"Which one?" said the car.

"How many are there?" Rutger asked.

"One. All songs only have one chorus. But they're all different in this song. The refrains, I mean."

Rutger flexed his jaw. "Play the last one."

Standing in a Styrofoam igloo, the Egg Man goes
"Flimflam! Flimflam! I am the Egg Man!"
And when the dawn cracks open, the Egg Man knows
it's time to scram (yeah yeah baby yeah yeah yeah).

"Stop. Put it in manual." He grabbed the steering wheel, looked over his shoulder, and backed out of the driveway.

Nice day out. Scattered clouds. 73 degrees. A gentle breeze. Smell of freshly cut grass. Smell of not altogether defiled lake water. He rolled the window down and stuck out his hand. His fingers quivered and flapped in the wind. He turned his hand over and let it ride the wind like a flaccid surfboard, like a breakdance move in slow motion.

The speed limit was 35 mph. Rutger was going 34 mph when he crashed into the telephone pole, two blocks from home.

"Uitroep," said the car.

A crowd of neighbors formed around the accident, instantly, as if they had been waiting for it. Ignoring everybody, Rutger got out and circled the BMW, sizing up the damage. It wasn't bad. The front fender was dinged a little. That appeared to be all.

A little boy in the crowd had a baseball bat. Rutger asked him for it. The boy said, "It's my bat."

Rutger took it.

He circled the car again, slowly, sticking out his neck and grimacing at the paint job. Then he whaled on the hood once, twice...

"Thanks kid." He threw the bat at its owner, got in the car and told it to drive him home.

The car reluctantly obeyed, complaining about its pain sensors and demanding an explanation for the attack.

———

Neo-Confucian Out-of-the-Corner-of-the-Mouthism

There are three reasons why a man elects to destroy his body. Number one: he is a man. Number two: no man will destroy a man who has already destroyed himself. Number three: destruction is inevitable. These are the days of our lives.

"Goodbye," Said Mr. Van Trout

"I'm going to staple my cheeks together." Nobody was in the room but Mr. Van Trout. He picked the stapler up from the desk. "Now I'm going to do it." He opened his mouth wide, wider, wider...He opened the stapler and fixed it to the outside of his cheeks. He swallowed a sheet of sandpaper. Carefully, bit by bit, he put pressure on the arms of the stapler... The tips of a staple pierced his cheek. A tear of blood fell down his face, traced his jawline, dripped off of his chin and splashed onto his shoe. He imagined his face coming together like the wings of a butterfly...He put down the stapler. "I can't do it." He licked a fingertip and wiped his wounded cheek. "I can't do it." He put a band-aid on the wound.

"Did I hear a band-aid?" said Mrs. Van Trout, poking her head into the room.

"Goodbye," said Mr. Van Trout.

———

Rutger Jr. looked in the mirror. "Grr," he said.

He ran a finger across his hairline. Was it getting thicker? Was it crawling down his forehead? He studied his brow, first with naked eyes, then with a magnifying glass. If he was going to turn into a werewolf, his brow would foretell the tale.

Everything seemed ok. No unibrow. Not even the faintest hint of peach fuzz between the two slashes of blond hair above his eyes. He remembered when Dr. Coots treated him for lycanthropy. The treatment consisted of mere electrolysis between the eyes. "One thing leads to another," Dr. Coots said. "Best nip this in the bud." Apparently the doctor had experienced a similar trauma as a teenager. "I even changed into a werewolf a few times." But once his unibrow was electrolysized, he told Rutger Jr., he ceased to exhibit lycanthropic behavior.

Still, Rutger Jr. suspected that he had werewolf blood. It was only a matter of time before the beast came out. He wondered how it would happen. Would he grow hair all over his body? Would his body physically change into a big monster? Or would he rip his skin off to reveal the monster underneath? He worried about it hurting. He didn't want to rip his skin off. What if it didn't grow back right? Would it even grow back, or would he have to rip the werewolf skin off of himself to get back to his real, human self? He would have to deal with it. That's the price of damnation.

In the meantime, Rutger Jr. decided to go eat a Ding Dong. He walked downstairs. On his way to the pantry he passed his father in the hallway. Rutger Sr. carried a suitcase and umbrella. "Where're you going, Dad?"

"Goodbye," said Mr. Van Trout.

———

Layke and a boy were making out in the garage. The boy had his hands up her shirt, awkwardly groping her breasts as he slurped on her mouth. Layke kissed him back with a thirty percent effort. Her arms hung lifelessly at her sides.

Rutger stared at them for a few seconds, then tiptoed across the garage towards the BMW Futique.

"Dad?"

He froze. For a moment he thought if he didn't move, nobody would see him. No such luck. The lights in the garage were on. Layke said, "Hey Dad. What're you doing?"

Straightening up, Rutger replied, "Nothing. What are you doing? Who's your friend?"

Layke looked at her partner. "Dunno. Some kid. I've never seen him before. I just came out here to get a soda from the fridge and one thing led to another."

The boy glanced back and forth between Rutger and Layke with an injured, fearful expression.

"Is that true, son?" Rutger intoned. "Are you taking advantage of my daughter? I hope not. So help me. What's your nationality? Are you biracial or is that a tan? It ain't Dutch—I know that much."

Agape, the boy turned to run away. He tripped over a toolbox, cartwheeled, hit a storage closet, bounced off it, stepped and slipped on a basketball, waved his arms, honked like a goose, and somersaulted out the back door of the garage in an ungainly bramble of limbs.

"Why'd you do that for!" cried Layke. "Thanks a lot."

Rutger bowed his head.

Layke said, "Hey Dad. Where'd you get that new car? It's new, right?"

"Goodbye," said Mr. Van Trout. He said it once to his daughter, and twice to his silo.

———

Rutger got lost on the way out of Quiggle Estates. The Vulgaria was a rhizomatous system of inlets, cul-de-sacs, alleyways and strip malls that spanned five miles in every direction from its nucleus, Quiggle Lake, a once remote body of water in the middle of a forest that now described the outer rim of the area's upper echelon McMansions. Depending on cloud cover, the surface of the lake shifted in color between an alien toxic green and a cold gunmetal gray. People fished in it regularly. Some people swam in the lake, even though the water contained a variety of flesh-eating diseases. But as a rule McMansionites experienced difficulty with cumulative thinking.

Forty minutes later, Rutger stumbled upon an entrance. At first he didn't know where he was. Nor did he know where he was going. Just away. Away from his family. Away from his neighbors. Away from Quiggle Estates and Vulgarias and the GRIM and Dutch people and even his beloved silo. Maybe he would go down to Ohio. Maybe further, like Argentina. He had never been to South America. He didn't know anything about South America. There was an entire world down there, bigger than the United States, much bigger, and nobody gave two shits about it. He imagined himself taking a six month journey around the coast. He imagined the mysterious cultures he would see, the green vistas he would enjoy, the cold beers he would drink...The cliffs, the rainforests. The giant statues of Virgin Mary and the flamenco dancers. Sombreros. *Pisco*...What else did South America have? Poor people. Stinking, congested cities. Cocaine...But he would stay clear of the cities. Maybe he wouldn't have a choice. Maybe South America was like North America and cities no longer existed except as the hangnail junctions of so many Vulgarian fingers...He could pull it off. No sweat. He had plenty of money readily available in at least six bank accounts that he could think of off the top of his head. There was work, of course, but he didn't need to go into the office to get things done. Had he ever even been into the office?...The BMW's computer was more than sufficient for all business purposes. The BMW, in fact, could do his work for him. It wasn't hard. Any person, place or thing could excel at his profession of choice given a set of simple how-to instructions...Despite Rutger's feelings of unsettledness, however, he loved his family. Layke. Francisco. Rutger Jr. They annoyed him. They irked him. He suspected they often plotted against him, individually and as a group. His wife the esoteric weirdo. His daughter the underhanded sex fiend. His son the overimaginative pussy...But he loved the sons of bitches. He even loved his house, and his job. And his silo.

South America faded from Rutger Van Trout's mind like a ghost at sunrise.

Ghost

To prepare for his role in *Ghost* (1990), Patrick Swayze trained in the same way that he did for his role in *Roadhouse* (1989): ripping the jugulars out of cattle. When asked why, he replied, "Why fix what ain't broke?" He said he liked to train in the morning as the sun crept over the jagged horizon of his Idaho ranch.

Swayze received a Golden Globe nomination for *Ghost*. He received no formal acclaim for *Roadhouse*, although the film did achieve swift cult status. In a posthumously published conversation with director Igsnay Bürdd on the set of *The Patrick Swayze Show* (March 2018 - April 2018), he retrospectively referred to the anomaly as an instance of Derridean différance in which a "force of signification" came back to "pay the piper." When asked to clarify, he replied, "Différance defies clarification. Its 'meaning' is always-already slipping away."

———

Mr. Van Trout thought: I need a new praying mantis.

His old praying mantis had died unexpectedly last week. Mrs. Van Trout probably poisoned it: usually he paid more attention to the bug than to her. Mr. Van Trout had no real affinity or preference for the bug. Staring at it for hours on end was just a hobby. There was something mesmerizing about its devout stance, its frontal legs clasped together in prayer. Every so often the bug rubbed its legs together as if sitting down to a hot meal, and sometimes it used the legs to smooth back the invisible hairdo on its bald, triangular head. Referred to by entomologists as the tyrannosaurus rex of the insect world, praying mantises had hypnotic gazes. Mr. Van Trout frequently got lost in his praying mantis' eyes, which appeared simultaneously vacant and full of purpose and meaning. He imagined they carried on entire conversations just by looking at each other. A ridiculous idea, of course. It was an insect and insects didn't converse. They killed and cannibalized. But nobody could tell for sure what was going on in the head of a praying mantis. Empathy is a fiction. Despite scientific evidence, a man can't truly feel or know what another thing does. A man only feels and knows his own subjectivity. Everything else is fertilizer.

There was a praying mantis store in Strip Mall Martindale on 28th Street. Downtown had better praying mantis stores, but he didn't feel like driving into the heart of the GRIM and dealing with traffic. Mantisland was just a mile or two away. Mr. Van Trout took his hands off the wheel and told the car where to go.

———

"Knock knock! Knock knock! Knock knock!" The man checked his watch and elevated his head. "Knock knock! Knock knock! Knock knock!" His voice echoed down the street.

Mrs. Van Trout cracked open the door and peeked outside. Her grin belonged to a jack-o-lantern. "Was that you screaming out here?"

"Physical actions are overrated," said the man.

Her grin dissolved, and she prodded a cheek with her tongue.

The man wore a beat up top hat and a long, dark overcoat with an astrakhan collar and cuffs. He carried a cane. His face was a luminescent barbershop pole whose stripes seemed to swirl up one moment, down the next. The pole was too thin to be a mask: only a shrunken head could fit in there. Was it an optical illusion? Or was this thing an android? Did Mrs. Van Trout live in a world that accommodated androids? She wasn't sure; she hadn't watched the news since childhood. Space operas were all she watched. "Where's your face?" she snapped. "Your physiognomy doesn't make sense."

"Physiognomy?" His voice creaked like a rusty windmill and seemed to emanate from his abdomen. "Who uses the word physiognomy? Are you trying to prove something? People who try to prove things wear their insecurities on their physiognomies."

Mrs. Van Trout opened the door all the way. "Excuse me?"

The man proceeded as if she had just opened the door. "Good afternoon, ma'am. My name is Mr. Blankety Blank. I'm new in the area and wanted to inform you that I will be executing a torrent of serial killings over the course of the next few months in Quiggle Estates. I'm obliged to let a certain percentage of the Vulgaria's residents know my intentions by decree of the GSKCC—translated Geneva Serial Killers Code of Conduct—which was ratified only last year. Hence my cold call. I hope you'll excuse this piece of abruptness and will not hold it against me as bodies and conspiracy theories begin to pile up. I can't say who I'll kill yet. Factually I have no idea. I've only introduced myself to a handful of residents so far and I'm still determining who I hate and don't hate as well as the nature of my psychopathy and morally challenged modus operandi. Well, that's all. Have a nice day." He tipped his head, pinched the rim of his hat, turned with a flap of his overcoat and marched away.

Suspecting her skeleton of foul play, Mrs. Van Trout shut the door.

——

Rutger told the car to park diagonally across two parking spaces. "But not too diagonally," he cautioned. He didn't want people to think that he was some well-heeled *Frederson* who worried about them opening their doors into his car and dinging it, which is to say, he didn't want people to think he was what he was. He just wanted to come off as a sloppy driver—the kind of driver who might open his door into somebody else's car and ding it. This, in addition to the dents in its hood, would ensure that people steered clear of his car.

A few old ladies glared fearfully at the BMW Futique and clutched their mouths as Rutger got out. Nodding at them, he hailed a mechanical rickshaw that wheeled him down the artificial cobblestone main drag of Strip Mall Martindale to the eighth exit and the first of three Mantisland entrances.

An irreality TV show was being filmed outside the entrance. Rutger had seen the show before. He couldn't remember its name. It might have been "The Show." He recognized the main character. He was the only character— an expressionless, nondescript male in his late 50s who traveled to different strips malls around Michigan, stood against their pseudobrick walls and, once an hour, on the hour, droned, "This is real." Intermittently he said, "This is reality," and it was the task of the audience, over the course of a month, to determine how many times the protagonist tacked on an *ity* to the word *real* and precisely where and why those aberrations took place in the temporal scheme of things. To do so successfully resulted in the breaking of a code that Rutger had always found too tedious to waste time on. But he had to admit liking the show. He liked it almost as much as staring at praying mantises.

Rutger goosed the cameraman as he passed behind him, then scurried into Mantisland. The cameraman glanced over his shoulders with confused, birdlike jerks.

Inside Mantisland the small, square aquariums rose to the ceiling and stretched across the expanse of rubber floor. Each aquarium contained one praying mantis of a particular species. Most of the insects were silent, static, petrified except for a twitch or sway of antennae. A few score of troublemakers, however, hissed and made spitting sounds. Sometimes they screamed.

Salesmen gravitated towards Rutger like paparazzi towards a movie star. "Sir!" they exclaimed, raising their fingers as they closed in. "Sir! Sir! Sir!"

"Back off, damn you!" Rutger clapped his hands and stomped his feet. "Back the fuck off, you damned mosquitoes!" He grabbed a broom leaning against a banister and smacked it against the ground while continuing to rant and curse. No effect. The salesmen's circular ranks continued to tighten like a sphincter. It wasn't until Rutger slammed one of them in the nose with the butt of the broom that they balked and retreated to their shadowy posts.

"Unkind," burbled the salesman who had been hit. Blood flowed into his mouth and down his chin. "Very unkind, sir."

Rutger tossed the broom aside. "Unkindness is like morality," he said. "Criminally subjective."

He browsed for over two hours before deciding on a *hierodula parviceps* or Philippine mantis. Nothing special. It had a slightly enlarged head and resembled a miniature stiletto boot. Basically it looked like all of the other praying mantises in the store. But this was the last one. Currently Mantisland had no other *hierodula parviceps* in stock, and they wouldn't restock them for at least a week. Rutger had to buy it now.

So did several other shoppers, apparently. Nobody was in sight at the outset, but when Rutger neared the prize, a handful of bottomfeeders appeared, as if they had been waiting for him to get his hopes up before making their move. They collapsed on the aquarium just before it was within his grasp. Rutger didn't flinch. He strode forward, yanked the aquarium out of their fumbling hands, and methodically kicked them in the groins. He met some success with this tactic, but his victims wised up quickly, blocking the kicks with assured karate chops. Then they retaliated. They punched him. They kneed and elbowed him. They tossed him around like an old ventriloquist doll. The praying mantis changed hands repeatedly. Things looked grim...until his oppressors suddenly, collectively fatigued and Rutger rose against and quashed them.

"I win," he wheezed in a tone that unintentionally sounded like THE VOICE.

Bruised, bleeding, hunched over—his sciatic nerve had given out again—Rutger journeyed to a cashier and paid for his merchandise.

"There you are, sir," chirped the cashier, securing the praying mantis in a cellophane bag.

"Goodbye," said Mr. Van Trout.

———

goodbye (gŏŏd-bī′)

1. An expression of farewell (alteration of *God be with you*).
2. Infamously opinionated quarterly journal of contemporary obituaries.
3. Surname of Hans Kilgore, McSubübermensch explorer and discoverer of regenerative peanut butter. Also holds the Guinness world record for Fastest Time to Pluck a Turkey (1 minute, 14 seconds).
4. Strain of South African pumpkin pie originating in Cape Town shortly after the decolonization of white power in the twentieth century.
5. In popular media, an album by Cream and Dubstar; a song by the Spice Girls, Gravity Kills and Granddaddy; and the name of an episode of British sitcom Black Adder (officially titled *Goodbyeee...*).
6. What the Von Trapp children say before retiring to bed.
7. Alternate means of saying "Adieu."

———

He opened the door, peeked inside. Walked inside.

He took off his shoes and hung up his keys.

He peeked into the kitchen, walked into the kitchen, and opened the refrigerator. Leftover meatballs. He poured leftover sauce on the meatballs, heated them up in a microwave, and ate them with a fork.

"Naptime." He rinsed the dirty dish and utensils. He left them in the sink.

His sciatic nerve smarted. But he refused to submit to the pain. He forced himself to walk upright.

A TV caught his eye on the way upstairs.

A black-and-white tornado ripped across the superscreen, scooping up tractors, farmers, livestock, outhouses, sheds...The host of the show was a man with a metallic, clicking voice.

He moved closer. He sat on the couch. Groaned.

"What're you watching here," he said to his son, who was entranced, who couldn't look away, who held an empty Ding Dong carton in one hand and a miniature holographic tornado in the open palm of his other hand.

"*Tornado Video Classics,*" the boy chirped. "I ordered it. Came with this little tornado. See?" He showed him. "It's called a multiple vortex tornado. Cool, huh?" He frowned. "What happened to you? You're bleeding."

He wiped his lips. He admired his knuckles. He put an arm around his son. "Got a new bug is all. Let's watch the rest of this show."

Sound of flapping wheat and corn stalks interspersed with exclamations of "Tarnation!"...

Contemporary Juwes

After slashing her throat, he rinsed the blood from the Buster sword in a stainless steel sink and waited for her to die. It didn't take long. He had cut her exactingly, deeply, down to the spine, and she dashed around the kitchen for half a minute like a chicken on fire, blood exiting her neckhole in thick, oily spurts. Finally she ran into a wall, threw her arms into the air, made a noise that sounded like a lawn mower running over a football, and collapsed into a quivering lump.

The lump stopped quivering.

He removed a quill from an inner pocket of his overcoat, knelt down, poked a hole in a clean patch of skin, watched it bleed, watched a small red pool expand across the floor tiles, and dabbed the tip of the quill in the blood. He changed his mind, put the quill away and took out a paint brush. He gathered some blood in a shot glass, stood, and wrote his name on the wall:

mr blankety blank

He admired the lettering, refining and touching it up in places.

Satisfied, he sprayed Windex on his head and squeak-cleaned it with a paper towel. Then he left.

———

Quote

"Believe me, if I started murdering people...there'd be none of you left."

   —Charles Manson, Cult Leader

———

A gleaming rollerball truck souped up with razorwire antennae, scores of shark fins, and edible vegecarbon tires squealed down Buttrick Ave. and claimed the lives of over twenty peregrinating animals, among them Siamese cats, wiener dogs, blue racers, skunks and raccoons. The roadkill lay untouched for hours before the children came home from school and began to play with it. They lit the more mangled corpses on fire. They picked up the other corpses by their tails and swung them over their heads like helicopter blades until they grew tired and passed out in a heap of young, hairless limbs or their acid-lipped mothers or Mr. Moms called them inside for dinner.

Dusk surged down the rooftops and flooded the streets.

Steam hissed from the roadkill, which grew cold, hard, bloodless...And then he stole across the street, overcoat flapping, head glowing and spinning... The roadkill grew warm, soft...oozing undead sap...

———

Quote

"Carcasses bleed at the sight of the murderer."

   —Robert Burton, Vicar

———

Mertle Underlay opened her eyes and looked at the clock. 9:00 p.m. Who rang the doorbell? Was it Halloween already? She looked over her shoulder. Her husband was dusting the epic bicep of a giant Thinker statue in the corner of the family room. "Who's at the door?" she asked.

Herman winced. "Dunno. I haven't been to the door."

"This doesn't make any sense." Mertle told her chair to stand up. Two mechanical legs sprung out of the arms. The chair stiffened and clumsily angled upwards, unloading Mertle onto her feet. She nearly fell down. She thwacked the chair with the jockey whip that she always kept close by her side, then strode across the room and thwacked her husband for no particular reason, then shouted at her identical triplet sisters in Kitchenette #2. "What's going on in there? Is that popcorn done or what? Why do you bitches always exclude me? It's not my fault I don't look like you! Get your asses out here!"

"Hold on!" one of the sisters hollered distantly. "Charlotte's walking on her hands!"

"Somebody's at the door!" Mertle wondered again if it was Halloween. It was October, she knew that. Late October. Had she forgotten Halloween again? Same thing happened last year. Kids started ding-donging and she didn't have any candy to shell out. So she gave children slices of Kraft cheese, and when the supply dried up, she handed out frozen dinners and miniature bottles of sparkling water. Rumor of her absentmindedness spread across Quiggle Estates and she had to endure the underhanded ridicule of her neighbors for a full year. Was she staring another year of petty bullshit in the face?

The question could have been answered by her husband. She was too angry at him to ask, though. Why was she angry at him? She couldn't remember...She might also go into the kitchen and ask her sisters. Or she could turn on the TV and watch the Calendar Channel. Or she could answer the front door and see who rang the doorbell. If there were children wearing costumes, it was probably Halloween (unless the children were merely practicing for Halloween, of course, which Mertle herself used to do). But if some costumeless person rang the doorbell, she may have been in the clear (although not necessarily, on the off-chance that a child or group of children, for instance, were dressed up as "normal children" and their costumes consisted of no costumes, that is, "normal clothes and hairdos"). But maybe the doorbell hadn't rung in the first place. She had been half asleep after all. Maybe the ring she heard—if she even heard a ring—had occurred in a hypnagogic dream. No way to tell. Actually there were multiple truth-telling strategies available to her. But which tactic would be the most effective?

Ding-dong.

So it wasn't a dream. Somebody was actually at the door. Unless, that is, her ears had played another trick on her.

She eyeballed Herman. "The doorbell. Sometimes it rings."

Herman squeezed behind the thinker statue. He rubbed and massaged the statue's bronze shoulders as if it were a boxer about to enter the ring. "Sometimes it rings," he confirmed.

"I asked you a question, dumbass." Mertle stomped the floor. Herman cowered, arguing that she didn't ask him a question. On the contrary, she made a statement. Mertle stormed across the room and whipped him again. Most of the blows fell on the statue.

She went to Kitchenette #2.

Charlotte was still walking on her hands. She scurried around the vast granite countertop of an island sink with legs hanging over her head like two meaty antennae as her lookalike sisters, Berlin and Sonya, halfheartedly cheered her on.

"Get off that counter!" Mertle shrieked. "Lansakes your hands are filthy! Look at those filthy hands!"

"I washed them two seconds ago," Charlotte replied as she negotiated a hulking stainless steel canister of sugar. Her sisters endorsed the claim with exaggerated, wide-eyed nods.

Crouching, Mertle leapt at Charlotte with catlike agility. She missed her target by a wide margin. Everybody watched her sail across Kitchenette #2 into the pantry closet. The door slammed shut behind her. There was a great crash of canned goods. The door opened and Mertle walked out dripping in chicken noodle soup. She cursed. She whipped the pantry door. She asked her sisters if they had heard the doorbell.

"Doorbell?" they said, frowning at one another as if the word was a neologism Mertle had just invented.

The doorbell rang again—faraway, but audible.

"There it is! There it is!" Mertle pointed. "Don't tell me you didn't hear that! Did you invite somebody over?"

"It's Halloween," Berlin lied. "We came over to celebrate with you. Why would we invite somebody over?" Sonya smacked her lips. Charlotte tumbled off the counter and said, "Did you forget Halloween again?"

"No," said Mertle defensively. She tried to whip her sisters. They knew her style, though, and expertly dodged and deflected her flyswats. Psychotic with frustration, Mertle retrieved a can of mushroom soup from the pantry. She sprinted to the front door, opened it, and threw the can at the figure standing on the porch. She missed. The can flew across her front lawn and nailed the mailbox, knocking it off its perch. "Holy crap!" she shouted. "I couldn't do that again if I tried!"

Mr. Blankety Blank glanced over his shoulder, then back at Mrs. Underlay. "But you didn't try."

Mertle made a face.

Mr. Blankety Blank ripped her face off with a pair of monofilament Krueger claws. Ten minutes later he clicked shut the Underlay's screened in porch, five faces neatly tucked into a satchel.

Quote

"I'm sorry I killed five people, ok?"
—Gary Allen Walker, Serial Killer

Lou Diamond Phillips took a delicate sip of green tea and admired the new window treatment in his living room. Noticing an errant string jutting out of the gossamer maroon curtain, he put down his tea and snipped the string off with a pair of nail cutters. He inspected the curtain for more irregularities, then opened it and looked out the window.

He clicked his jaw.

Something in his front yard. A scarecrow. Possibly a human-sized crow. Its nondescript head glowed the glow of a fever dream.

The figure started to juggle...five objects. Lou thought the objects were raw chicken skins, maybe deflated Cornish hens, but when he turned the lights on, he saw that they were something else.

He recalled a moment from the set of *Interface* (1984), his first film, in which he played the role of Punk 1. He had been practicing a complex facial expression when Roggie Cale (Punk 3) broke onto the set, drunk and ornery and in possession of three dead chickens. He proceeded to juggle the chickens. Eventually he skinned them with a survival knife as the entire cast and crew looked on in confusion. How old had he been then? Twenty-two? Twenty-three?

Lou left the window and ambled to the front door, choking on a lump of nostalgia.

He opened the door. Artificial lightning bugs swam through the darkness, their motors greased and silent.

Quote

"When childhood dies, its corpses are called adults."

—Sir Brian Aldiss, Science Fiction Author

Mr. Vandermuelen turned to the Channel Channel and flipped through the 10,098 station holodex. Every year he purchased hundreds of new channels, and yet the more he acquired, the less shows seemed to be on, not to mention that it became increasingly tedious to search through the holodex and try to find something worthwhile. Usually, by the time he found a show to watch, it was already over. Tonight he decided to use the *I Ching*. Clearing his mind, he dumped a canister of yarrow stalks onto the carpet and sifted through them.

He constructed a hexagram and asked a blowup Lao T'zu doll what it meant.

"K'un," said the doll. "There is no water in the lake. The image of exhaustion. Thus the superior man stakes his life on following his will. No blame. When one has something to say, it is not believed."

Stroking his chin, Mr. Vandermuelen contemplated the judgment.

The holodex spun like a roulette wheel and he made a selection.

Channel 14,901. USA (Übermensch Sitcoms of Americana) 8. "The Will to Shower." Starting time: 4:04. Duration: 404 minutes. Current time: 4:04.

Excited by the synchronicity, Mr. Vandermuelen focused intently on the wall-screen, sipping a dirty Manhattan.

He turned off the TV thirty-six minutes later.

"The Will to Shower" was unsatisfactory. So were most of the shows on USA 8. They all featured ridiculously mundane Spanish protagonists in ridiculously mundane situations (sometimes fictional, sometimes nonfictional) who had to overcome being ridiculously mundane in some way. In "The Will to Shower," the protagonist had to overcome a severe case of hydrophobia (fear of water) and enter a shower to wash himself. After the opening credits, pop songs and schizercials, the camera settled into an extreme close-up of the protagonist's pock-marked face. His expression changed slightly every ten to twenty seconds as he considered what to do. Now and then he said something in Spanish (e.g. "Pregunto qué hacer") or German (e.g. "Ich bin für Suppe hungrig"). Aside from a few gratuitous penis shots, this accounted for the bulk of the action in the sitcom. Mr. Vandermuelen had seen the episode before and knew what happened in the end: the protagonist turned the shower on, stepped in, began to clean himself, began to whistle the theme song for Irish Spring soap, and abruptly melted like the Wicked Witch of the West into a gory pool of green, roach-infested slime. As the protagonist suspected, the water had been deathly acidic all along. Not a bad climax. But not worth the wait.

The wall-screen folded into a small hole in the wall. The hole in the wall spit out an animated, science fictional version of René Magritte's painting Golconde. Identical neobourgeois men in facemasks and jetpacks fell onto a Fritzlangian metropolis like raindrops. Mr. Vandermuelen stared at the painting and sipped his Manhattan at deliberate intervals.

The phone rang. Mr. Vandermuelen said, "Pick up," before the first ring had elapsed.

"Hello?"

"Hello, sir. How are you this evening?"

Telemarketer. But Mr. Vandermuelen didn't have anything else to do. "Fine," he droned.

"That's nice. My name is Brent Bowtie. I'm calling on behalf of USA 8 to ask why you changed the channel during 'The Will to Shower' after watching only thirty-six minutes of the show."

"What?"

Brent Bowtie introduced himself again, told him what he wanted again.

Mr. Vandermuelen sat up in his chair. "What?"

Brent Bowtie repeated himself.

"Who are you?"

"I'm Brent Bowtie"

"Brent Bowtie?"

"That's me. That's my name."

"You're calling me because I changed the channel?"

"You changed it."

"Brent Bowtie?"

Dead air.

Mr. Vandermuelen said, "Are you watching me watch TV?"

"Of course, sir. Somebody's watching me watch you, too. And somebody's watching him. And so on. I'm right outside your house in a van. There's a bigger van parked behind me. There's an even bigger van behind that one. And so on. We all have telescopes. Do you understand?"

"No." Mr. Vandermuelen looked out the window.

"That's ok. The point is, we want to make sure our viewers are content. More importantly, we want to make sure they don't change the channel during one of our shows. So, again, I'm wondering why you changed the channel during 'The Will to Shower.' Did you not like the show?"

He didn't see anything. There was an overturned tricycle in the street. But no vans. "No, I didn't. And I didn't change the channel. I turned off the TV."

"Oh. Do you not like TV?"

Dead air.

"Well, let me ask you this, if it's not too much to ask. Why did you turn off the TV? Did it have something to do with the show?"

"Yes."

"It did?"

"Yes. It did."

"Oh no." Brent Bowtie began to cry. Then the line went dead.

———

Quote

"There is no happiness without tears, no life without death. Beware: I am going to make you cry."

—Lucian Staniak, Serial Killer

———

Six blocks away from Trent Vandermuelen's McMansion, a delivery man sped down Cascade Road on a motorized unicycle towards Harry Bombgarten's McMansion to drop off a pizza. The man was upset. Who ordered pizza with chocolate-cherry frosting on it? More importantly, who ordered pizza with sentient pepperoni? Both items had devogued long ago, and it unnerved the delivery man to think that somebody thought they were being cool when in reality their fashion sense hinged on ignorance or some kind of retrograde, I-want-to-be-kitschy wistfulness. He imagined the creatively foul-mouthed ways he might tell the client off when he reached his destination.

A black, flapping blur whooshed out of the darkness and tackled the delivery man. He flew into somebody's Astroturf yard and tumbled into an out-of-season nativity scene, knocking the plastic players over like bowling pins. The unicycle fell onto its side and screeched across the street in a cloud of sparks. The pizza carton leapt straight into the air, flipping end over end, and landed on its backside with a resounding smack. For a moment everything was still, silent. Then the top of the pizza carton snapped open and the pepperonis inside began to squeak and gibber. They crawled out of the morass of frosting like creatures from a swamp and inched across the asphalt, twitching, trying to shake the frosting from their hides.

A Liston knife glinted in the light of a streetlamp.

Mr. Blankety Blank fell on the pepperonis. Hacking madly and indiscriminately, he sliced them into smaller parts. The pepperonis squealed. They bled. But they didn't die; their residual fragments became individuals with minds of their own. All the killer effectively did was hurt them. No matter how small the cut, he couldn't kill them. Even a hair-sized slice of pepperoni formed its own personality. As promised in the pizza shop's well-known schizercial, "Only the pot can perish the pepperoni," which is to say, only human stomach acid could put them to death.

Flustered, Mr. Blankety Blank hacked off the delivery man's knees and used them to make clip-clopping noises as he galloped down the street.

———

Quote

"I didn't want to hurt them. I only wanted to kill them."

    —David Berkowitz, Serial Killer

———

Billy Ray Royerson entered the kitchen and chewed on his thumb and observed the swaying backside of a bent-over Rosie the Robot cleaning a patch of dirt off of the thermal acrylic kitchen floor and shortly he began to contemplate all the places he had been and all the money he had made and all the women he had taken advantage of and all the potential bastards he had fathered and it felt good to stand there in his kitchen and be himself this man this maestro this middle-aged dynamo with a power chin that didn't quit and then a serial killer strolled into the kitchen dribbling his wife's severed head like a basketball and shooting it into the sink for a three pointer and when Billy Ray saw his wife's round accusing eyes he roared and hurled knives at the killer one after another he pulled them out of an arty block of oak with a metallic unsheathing sound butcher's knives dinner knives Ginsu knives machetes but nothing hit its target and ten seconds later the killer stood over him pulling two thumbs out of his eye sockets.

———

Quote

"People commonly travel the world over to see rivers and mountains, new stars, garish birds, freak fish, grotesque breeds of human; they fall into an animal stupor that gapes at existence and they think they have seen something."

—Søren Kierkegaard, Philosopher

———

They called him Defenestration Jones. His family called him DJ Windowpain.

By day he worked as a local retail psychocritic, traveling from strip mall to strip mall and writing personality profiles on salespeople for publication in *The Quiggling Bean*, the Vulgaria's leading newspaper. By night he worked as a husband and father for a wife and kids who liked to make fun of him for being a local retail psychocritic as well as a closet homosexual and, above all, a window jumper.

It happened about once a month. The synapses in DJ Windowpain's brain misfired, causing him to march up the stairway of his McMansion to the fifth floor, open the window at the end of the hallway, and leap out of it...and leap out of it...and leap out of it...

The drop wasn't short. At the bottom, though, a brambly, defenestration-friendly Bonsai bush broke his fall and springboarded him across the lawn.

Then DJ Windowpain got up, dusted himself off, and marched back upstairs for another jump. And he kept jumping until fatigue or a broken bone prohibited him from jumping again.

That night, Mr. Blankety Blank passed by the Jones' McMansion during one of these defenestrative spectacles. He paused on the sidewalk. He stared.

DJ Windowpain's family and a few neighbors stood in the yard looking up at him as he announced his sixteenth jump of the evening and took the plunge. He leapt too far out, missed the bush, landed on his feet, and sprained an ankle. "You stupid idiot!" shouted Mrs. Jones. DJ Windowpain got to his feet and limped back to the house, grimacing in pain. His children oscillated between laughing and crying. The neighbors took photos and shot footage.

A few minutes later, the Gamehater made the scene. He regarded Mr. Blankety Blank suspiciously, wondering if he was a new superhero. He complimented the stranger on his outfit in hopes of starting a conversation. Mr. Blankety Blank ignored him. The Gamehater shrugged and approached Mrs. Jones. "Anything I can do ma'am?" He crossed his arms over a putty-padded chest.

Mrs. Jones looked the Gamehater up and down. She winced in disgust. "What're you in third grade?" she snorted. "Are you having sex with my husband?"

The Gamehater felt naked. He felt like he did as a boy when he got a boner in school between classes and had to walk down the hallway with a stack of books shielding his crotch. His giant plastic grin wavered, but he maintained composure, reassuring himself, again and again: "Don't hate the player. Don't hate the player. Don't hate the player..."

DJ Windowpain jumped a seventeenth time, landed on his head, and broke his neck.

"Now you need a new neck!" screamed his wife. The children threw themselves to the ground in an attempt to imitate their father. The neighbors threw themselves to the ground in an attempt to imitate the children.

Mr. Blankety Blank disappeared in the shadow of a fluid, fluttering veronica.

———

Quote

"You'll never get me. I'll kill again. Then you'll have another long trial. And then I'll do it again."

—Henry Brisbon, Serial Killer

———

Mr. Vandermuelen listened to the sound of the dead line and told the phone to hang up. Unable to think of anything else to do, he went to bed.

In the bathroom he popped a brush-bug into his mouth and stared at his image in the mirror while it cleaned his teeth. His cheeks poked out as if jabbed from the inside with toothpicks.

He bent over, spit the brush-bug into the sink...and shuddered at the sight of another reflection in the mirror.

He turned and faced the intruder. "Who are you? What's that? Is that some kind of sci-fi weapon? You can't bring a sci-fi weapon into my home."

Mr. Blankety Blank aimed the scramble gun at his victim...

Mr. Vandermuelen turned inside out, his organs and bones pinned to his skinsuit like tails on a donkey...Mr. Blankety Blank used a steak knife to slice off his liver and kidneys. He went downstairs to the kitchen, put a frying pan on the stove, and rummaged through the refrigerator. He took out three bottles of marinade. Each was a different brand and a different flavor. He regarded the marinades one at a time, uncertain of how to proceed.

———

Quote

"How shall I marinade my tenderloin this evening?"

—Albert Fish, Serial Killer

———

Dr. Skidmore Pachulski put on a devil's costume—red face, goatee, horns, cape, barbed tail, hooves, pitchfork...Halloween wasn't until Friday.

Henrietta Pachulski choked on a peach pit when her husband snuck up behind her and playfully jabbed her in the ass with the pitchfork. He tried to do the Heimlich maneuver. It didn't work. Knowing she was about to die, she threw a fountain pen at Skidmore out of spite. The pen struck him in the eye, and all of its ink unloaded into his brain.

The couple hit the floor at the same time.

Mr. Blankety Blank appeared three hours later. He removed the pen from Dr. Pachulski's eye and wrote a grocery list on one of his gloves. Then he dragged the Pachulski's corpses into the yard, disemboweled them, and formulated another message on their garage door with a fresh coat of blood.

———

Quote

"Probably the toughest time in anyone's life is when you have to murder a loved one because they're the devil."

—Emo Philips, Standup Comedian

———

A line of children stretched out from the window of an ice cream truck like a discarded umbilical cord.

Rutger Van Trout cut in line, making at least ten children behind him cry. He waited fifteen seconds, grew impatient, and muscled his way to the front of the line, nudging children out of the way. The ice cream man looked at him disapprovingly and said, "The only emperor is the emperor of ice cream."

"One popsicle, please," replied Mr. Van Trout. "Grape."

Tears welled up in the street and flowed into the gutters.

Mr. Van Trout shifted the BMW Futique into KITT mode and told it to take him home. The red Cylon eye on the grill illuminated and roamed back and forth. An old-fashioned loudspeaker emerged from the roof of the car and blasted the *Knight Rider* theme song. The residents of Quiggle Estates covered their ears, shouted obscenities, and hurled pieces of yard art at the BMW Futique as it passed them by.

Mr. Van Trout had just finished his popsicle when he passed by the Pachulski's house. A crowd had gathered outside. People in robes and business suits commingled and ran in circles. The sirens of police cars, ambulances, news vans flickered, blared and beeped. There were screams. There were animé eyes. He told the car to be quiet and park. He got out. He walked towards the house on his tiptoes, peeking over the heads of his neighbors.

A policeman stopped him.

"What's going on?" said Mr. Van Trout.

The policeman sighed. He gestured at the Pachulski's garage.

Mr. Van Trout squinted and tried to stand taller on his tiptoes. His calves hurt. "I can't see anything!" Fortunately the policeman was built like a professional wrestler. He walked behind Mr. Van Trout, picked him up by the shoulders, and held him there for a count of ten.

He saw it now. Scrawled across the garage door in giant letters.

the juwes are the men
that will not be blamed for nothing

The policeman set Mr. Van Trout down. Mr. Van Trout looked at the policeman and shook his head. "You ain't much if you ain't Dutch," he said.

———

Quote

"Blank blank blank blankety blank."

—Jack the Ripper, Serial Killer

Sausage Party

Barbara Flintlock asked the TV to mute. The TV asked why. Barbara said she didn't need to give a reason. The TV grumbled something, then muted.

Breathing deeply, she reached for the phone sensor.

Her hand was shaking. She pulled it back.

She reached for the sensor again. The hand continued to shake.

She pulled it back again, reached for the sensor again. Still the hand shook.

She knelt down and rested the hand on a coffee table. It fluttered like a bird that had been nailed to a tree stump. She stared at the hand. Now she knew what Wing Biddlebaum felt like. But serial killers made her nervous.

She stood up.

She reached for the sensor.

Her thumb and pinky finger flapped like wings and lifted her off of her feet.

———

Newsflash

In a creaking, scratchy Redrum voice: "Good morning Quiggle Estates. We interrupt the current irreality TV show to bring you the following newsflash... *Murder*. Murder most foul, as in the best it is, but this most foul strange and unnatural...Yesterday Quiggle Estates suffered the loss of at least 14 of its residents in a pileup of serial killings the likes of which hasn't been witnessed since the Johnnycake Tapdance murders of the early 20s. The rhizome of life that is our beloved Vulgaria is under siege. As of yet, GRIM police are clueless as to the identity of the killer or killers, this notwithstanding the vast abundance of clues that the killer or killers left behind. 'Sometimes there aren't enough clues,' GRIM Assistant Commissioner-in-Chief Sluman Bailey said at a spur-of-the-moment meeting on the corner of Snow Road and Thornapple River Drive this morning. 'In this case there are too many clues. It's confusing. We don't know where to start. All we can say is that the perpetrator of these murders is mean and fights dirty.' While additional murders are expected to be discovered throughout the day, the current shortlist of victims include blankety blank blank blankety blankety blank blankety blank blank blank. Indie newsman Brent Bowtie is also rumored to be dead, although some of his body parts are still unaccounted for. Additional victims include a family of sentient pepperonis who, thankfully, survived the gruesome attack. Of course, they'll never be the same, physically or psychologically. In the immortal words of Oral Sex a.k.a. Axl Rose: 'Where do we go now?' And now back to our regularly scheduled blankety blankety blank."

———

A group of families convened in S. Ingleby Erwin's back yard to cook sausages and get drunk. Everybody stood around their host in a circle holding beer cans and raw sausages. The children had been herded together in the Erwin's basement, shackled by the wrists and ankles, and muzzled with S&M Super Ball gags so that they wouldn't disturb their parents. The wide eyes of the children remained glossy with moisture throughout the afternoon. Few of them cried outright.

"Heck of a day, isn't it?" said Mr. Erwin. He freeze-framed an overzealous grin. The grin abruptly vanished. "Let's begin."

His guests cracked open their beers and chugged them, then had an *ad lib* belching contest.

Then they turned to Mr. Erwin and hurled their sausages at him.

He endured the spectacle of aggression—a host must always pay the price of being a host, however strange and unusual that price is—with dignity and grace, if not downright benevolence, making sure that each sausage hit him squarely, and encouraging guests who missed him to try again. When it was over, he collected the sausages from the Astroturf of his back yard. He spit-shined them individually and arranged them on an expansive Napoleon Prestige XLV Infrared grill as the guests lined up behind tall designer coolers to get more beer.

Barbara Flintlock lit a long cigarette and took a dramatic drag. Her hands shook wildly. "We're moving. I'm scared. I can't take this."

Conrad Flintlock reached around her neck and flicked the cigarette from her fingers. "Quit smoking. You're chainsmoking. You're a maniac."

"Leave her be, Conrad," said Connie Veneklausen.

"You leave her be. Go get remarried." He finished a beer, dropped it on the patio, and stomped on it.

"You get remarried," replied Mz. Veneklausen.

Lou Diamond Phillips said, "I'll marry you."

Mz. Veneklausen looked the old man up and down. "No thanks. I'm not into necrophilia. No offense."

"That wasn't very friendly of you," mumbled Mr. Phillips.

"Being friendly is for the birds."

"Are birds friendly with each other?" Miriam MacVengeance asked. "Are they even intelligent enough to know what friends are? Bird brains are tiny. They're like pinpricks. That's why people use the derogatory expression: 'So-and-so has bird brains.' Birds are dumbasses."

"You're a dumbass," said Job MacVengeance. His wife smirked and kicked him in the balls. He squealed. He squeezed his beer and toppled onto the Astroturf, gripping his crotch. Miriam dumped her beer on him, threw the empty beer can at him, and kicked him again, this time in the face. He lost consciousness.

"Jesus, Miriam," said Ed Adrian. He placed a hand over his private parts, as if to ensure the private parts that nothing like that would happen to them.

Mrs. MacVengeance got another beer from a cooler. "Spare me. We could all use a break from that asshole."

"He was just standing there," said Veronica Adrian. She ribbed her husband and growled, "Get your hand off your dick."

"Anyway," said Mrs. MacVengeance, and sipped her new beer.

Mrs. Flintlock lit another cigarette. "*Anyway*, like I was saying, I'm scared. Aren't you people scared?"

"Of what?" said Sig Zeeland, observing a vein in his forearm. He swiveled his wrist and made the vein squiggle.

"Of what?" said Mrs. Flintlock, dumbfounded. "Of dying. Of being disemboweled. Of being murdered and peed on. What do you think I mean?"

"Actually I heard the killer didn't urinate on anybody," said Mr. Adrian. "He urinated in a cup and cooked it in the microwave."

"You want something to be afraid of, check this out." Mr. Zeeland tore off his shirt in an animalistic fit of Hulkamania and began to strike poses. His wife Frieda tore her shirt off and followed suit. As they posed, they tried to nudge each other out of the way. Their shredded, anabolically pumped up physiques were works of fine art. Regular testosterone injections had rendered Mrs. Zeeland's naked chest the spitting image of her husband's.

"Who wants a sausage!" yelled Mr. Erwin. Everybody preferred their meat extra crispy and shook their heads no, except for John and Jane Smith, who politely raised their hands. Nodding, Mr. Erwin flung two medium-rare sausages at them with a fork. They struck the Smiths and fell on the ground. The Smiths picked the sausages up, brushed them off. Mrs. Smith took a leery bite. Mr. Smith retired to a condiment table.

"I'm not even sure anybody was killed yesterday," said Mr. Phillips. "Don't believe everything you see on the TV. Believe me."

"I'm not talking about the TV," huffed Mrs. MacVengeance. "I'm talking about what I saw with my own two eyes. I saw the blood. I saw the bodies. I even saw the killer. He's tall. He dresses like Zorro. Or Sherlock Holmes, maybe. Only he has a barbershop pole for a head. It swirls and everything."

"I saw that asshole," said Mr. Flintlock, and finished a beer.

"So did I," said Mz. Veneklausen, and finished a beer.

"Me too, I think," said Mr. Phillips, and finished a beer. "He was in my front yard the other night juggling chicken skins."

Jane Smith finished a beer, burped, and added, "He was at my front door the other day. Told me he was a serial killer. Told me he was planning a killing spree. Then he left. I thought it was a joke, but he did the same thing to a bunch of people. Craziness."

"I'm familiar with this gamester as well," said the Gamehater. The superhero had been hiding in a bush, waiting for the right moment to come out and crash the party. He placed fists on hips and pushed out his chest. Leaves snowed from his body. "I mistook him for another superhero. It wasn't until later, after I had taken off my disguise and returned to Clarkkenthood, that I realized something was amiss."

"Amiss?" Ed Adrian's forehead creased. "Who uses that word? Medievalites, that's who. And octogenarians."

The Gamehater said, "I don't know what the word octogenarian means. Medievalites, on the other hand, are people who existed during the medieval era, or, as it were, the 'middle ages.' The Latin derivation of medieval is 'medium' (as in *medi*) 'age' (as in *aev*)."

Mr. Adrian glared at him.

"The point is, had I known the gamester was a serial killer, I would have hated him. I would have hated him with extreme prejudice." He smiled. He swiveled his head, exhibiting another profile, and stretched out his arms. Today's costume was a black ensemble made of retread tires with crumpled aluminum trim and a crooked **GH** insignia splattered onto the chest. For a mask, he cut two eyeholes into a dampened Candyland board and wrapped it around his head. He looked like a car wreck. Everybody ignored him, although Mr. Erwin, embarrassed for the Gamehater (even though the Gamehater never seemed to be embarrassed by himself), did hurl a sausage at him.

"I have to take a leak," Mr. Smith announced. Mr. Erwin told him there were no public toilets in his McMansion. They argued.

Mr. Smith urinated on a colossal palm tree that rose out of the middle of the Erwin's back yard.

Mrs. Smith said, "What's the killer's name?"

"Blankety Blank," said Mz. Veneklausen.

"Blankety blank you, Connie," said Mrs. Smith.

"No, that's his name," said Mr. Phillips. "Mr. Blankety Blank. He wrote it on his first victim's wall."

"Oh."

"Yeah," chimed in Mrs. Zeeland, winded from posing and jockeying for position with her husband. "And he wrote something about Jews on his last victim's garage door. Mr. Blankety Blank's an anti-Semite."

"There's too many carbs in this beer!" screamed Mr. Zeeland as he scrutinized the nutrition index on a can. "Hey Erwin! Fuck're the protein drinks? I thought you were gonna pick some up!"

A sausage struck Mr. Zeeland in the back of the head.

"He's not an anti-Semite," said the Gamehater. "He's alluding to a message Jack the Ripper wrote on a wall after murdering Catherine Eddowes, his fourth victim according to most theorists on the subject. It's the same message, in fact."

Everybody looked askance at the Gamehater. "How do you know that?" asked Mrs. Erwin.

The Gamehater did an awkward jig. "One of my lesser known powers is Ripperology."

———

A Short History of Ripperology

The first documented emergence of a Ripperologist onto the stage of life occurred over two centuries prior to the 1888 emergence of Jack the Ripper in Whitechapel, London. Björn Hàmundarson, a celebrated Icelandic alchemist and magician, lost his ability to turn lead into gold, which is to say, he lost the ability to create the illusion of turning lead into gold. Why this happened is unknown except for one revealing entry from Hámundarson's diary, which he affectionately referred to as "Boss," and which was posthumously titled *Saga of the Magic Man (Try Try to Understand)*. Dated 24 July 1672, the passage reads:

Dear Boss:

Oi!

I can't remember how to deceive people. The villagers are going to stone me. I deserve it. Who forgets how to deceive people? Not to mention I've contracted stagefright, too.

It's the middle of summer and I'm freezing my balls off. Greenland's a lot warmer—don't believe what they tell you. I should move there. I might.

Yours truly,

G.H.[2]

Six inconsequential entries later, the diary ends. The ex-alchemist/ magician's many biographers, however, tell us that Hámundarson, alienated by his peculiar mnemonic inadequacy, had a psychotic breakdown, the effects of which manifested in various public displays of assholery. These displays included drunkenness, micturition, streaking, impulsive skullduggery, dropping firecrackers down the town crier's pants, impersonating the village idiot, swinging dogs over his head by their tails, and, above all, tearing Bibles in half. Every Sunday he waited outside church. When the bell clanged and the congregation dispersed, he tackled an indiscriminate churchgoer, confiscated his Bible, and ripped it to confetti with primitive cast-iron "scissorhands" (later extrapolated by Tim Burton in his film of the same name). Then Hámundarson ran into the woods. This went on for eighteen consecutive Sundays before the criminal was apprehended, tried and hung. During that period he developed a cult following and came to be known as "Björn the Bible Ripper," a nickname coined by blacksmith Egill Laxness, who himself came to be known as the first "Ripperologist" in light of the conspiracy theories he concocted and promulgated regarding the reasons for Hámundarson's arcane behavior. After his incarceration, authorities

---

2 Translated from Old Norse by Stanley Ashenbach.

questioned Hámundarson repeatedly about this behavior, but he pled the fifth with the same gusto he used to tear up Bibles, occasionally exclaiming, "I'm just a man," with Bartlebylike enthusiasm.

Fueled by Laxness and an infectious community of glib-lipped Ripperologists, conspiracy theories spiraled out of control in the wake of Björn Hámundarson's death. They persisted long after Laxness' own death, reaching across the geothermal expanse of Iceland and leaping over the ocean onto the southern tip of Greenland and most of Scandinavia. The theories sputtered out and died, however, before penetrating the convoluted social matrices of Great Britain and Western Europe. Not until the late nineteenth century did another strain of Ripperologists surface, albeit the term "Ripperologist" wasn't officially coined in this context until 1972, by Colin Wilson, who used it to implicate truth-seekers of the still unknown identity of Jack the Ripper. In an introduction to *Jack the Ripper: A Bibliography and Review of the Literature*, Wilson writes: "If investigation of Michael Harrison's theory proved that J.K. Stephen was Jack the Ripper, then the present bibliography of works on the Ripper would be, I assume, complete and the Ripper file would be closed. A sad but exciting day for Ripperologists, and a personal triumph for the compiler of the volume you are now holding in your hand."

Thereafter the term appeared in increasing numbers. Mainly it applied to practitioners of Ripper study and culture, but its application eventually fell on people who had nothing better to do with their time than waste it on trivial pursuits, ranging from historical analysis to unabashed loafing, dereliction, and green-eggs-and-ham-eating. "I may be lazy, but at least I'm no Ripperologist," became a global aphorism uttered by thousands on any given day. Whereas negative connotations of the term have weathered to some degree—Ripperology has been associated with superheroes, for instance—its articulation continues to incite dirty looks, pursed lips, accusatory tongues, and other physiognomic contractions, if not because of its somewhat antiquated association with sloth (and, for that matter, superheroes), but because people have ceased to understand or care about what it means.

―――

Down in the basement of the Ingleby's McMansion, Maisy Lyn Flintlock began to cry. The other children told her to shut up and take her medicine like a man, but their muzzles prohibited them from making any sense, and they only succeeded in slobbering all over themselves. Had she heard what was being said to her, she might have replied, "But I'm a girl," and the other children, in turn, might have replied, "Just because you're a girl doesn't mean you can't take your medicine like a man." In any event, soon Maisy Lyn stopped crying and the basement grew quiet again.

―――

Conrad Flintlock was machinegunned by a fusillade of sausages. He put up a good fight, but the sausages were too hard, too heavy, and they knocked him off of his feet. He stood, collected the sausages in his shirt, and hurried to a condiment table in a drunken zigzag.

The Gamehater had been talking for ten minutes without pause. During that time, most of the Erwin's guests pounded at least four more beers, except the Zeelands, who recommenced posing. Still, they listened to the Gamehater. It was the first time he could remember anybody listening to him in years. Even his chiropractic patients didn't listen to him. If he told them not to crack their necks, they cracked their necks. If he told them to take a certain medication, they didn't take the medication, or they took the wrong medication. Sometimes he felt like the entire universe had been created solely for the reason of opposing him. But not now. "*Jews* was spelled *J-u-w-e-s*," the Gamehater explained. "In the case of the Whitechapel murder, the message was ordered to be erased from the wall that Jack the Ripper allegedly scribbled it on. Police Commissioner Charles Warren worried that a riot would ensue if people got a load of the message, especially resident Jews. By the time the photographer showed up, it was gone. But it was recorded beforehand and has been a source of endless controversy."

On her way to a cooler, Miriam MacVengeance tripped over the lifeless body of her husband. Mr. MacVengeance woke up, mumbled something about a football game he had lost money on, and tried to stand. His wife kicked him unconscious again.

The Gamehater continued, "Nevertheless, a number of hypotheses surround the use of the misspelled *Juwes*. Some simply thought Jack was a stupid person who didn't know how to spell. In their minds he was an anti-Semite. Others thought he wanted people to believe that he was a stupid person and an anti-Semite. They say he did this for a variety of reasons. One reason is that he wanted to fuck with people, period. Another reason is that he wanted people to think a stupid Jewish person did the murders so as to divert attention from himself; more specifically, he wanted to unleash London society's latent anti-Semitism, although in retrospect there was nothing latent about it. Another reason is that he enjoyed the act of creating grammatical chaos, that is, of creating a metaphorical violence that reflected the actual violence he inflicted on whores, something that only a stupid Jewish person would partake in, as he saw it. Another reason is that he was Jewish and stupid and he wanted people to believe a stupid Jewish person could kill people just like a non-stupid, non-Jewish person. And so forth. And so forth. And so forth. And so forth. And so for—"

Mr. Smith punched the Gamehater in the face, denting the Candyland board. The Gamehater said, "Excuse me. Sometimes the record skips, as they say. Thank you. At any rate, a more probable explanation for the misspelled *Juwes* concerns a secret society of masons. Some Ripperologists believe the prostitutes were killed in the spirit of Masonic ritual. It's a long story. Once upon a biblical time there were these apprentice Masons named Jubela, Jubelo and Jubelum, three assholes who murdered a Masonic Grand Master, Hiram Abiff, shortly after he had built Solomon's Temple. They murdered him because he wouldn't tell them a secret. The content of this secret remains a secret. But that's beside the point. Jubela, Jubelo and Jubelum were busted and executed in a rather curious way: a strongman tore open their chests, took out their hearts and vital parts, and tossed the innards over his left shoulder like a handful of spilled salt. This execution is said to be laden with meaning, and it is this meaning that Jack the Ripper, a diehard Mason himself, harnessed to enact the Whitechapel murders. *J-u-w-e-s*, in other words, is not intended to be an anti-Semitic wisecrack, but rather an explicit reference to Jubela, Jubelo and Jubelum—the Juwes of Masonic lore. Now you're probably asking yourselves why Jack the Ripper killed a bunch of sluts to make an allegedly symbolic point about Masonic history and perhaps urban culture and the condition of—"

"This is boring!" interrupted Mrs. Adrian. "Who invited you anyway?" Beer frothed in the corners of her mouth as she spoke.

"I crashed," said the Gamehater in a confused, I-thought-crashing-a-party-was-perfectly-acceptable tone. He looked to others for support.

The Smiths urinated in a bush.

Connie Veneklausen jumped rope.

Lou Diamond Phillips talked to himself in a Puerto Rican accent à la his character in the 1988 film *Stand and Deliver*.

Sig and Frieda Zeeland took turns injecting steroids into each other's asses with dermal guns.

The Flintlocks and Ed Adrian busied themselves with a beer bong.

Miriam MacVengeance stared at the Gamehater hatefully.

Mr. Erwin continued to work the grill, flipping sausages two stories in the air. Mrs. Erwin had disappeared into the house.

Undeterred, the Gamehater pressed on. "What was I saying? Ah yes. History. Symbolism..."

Mrs. MacVengeance said, "He has a barbershop pole for a head. What is he, like, the Barber of Seville? What happened in *The Barber of Seville*? Was that a song? Wasn't that a Bugs Bunny cartoon? The one where he rubbed hair tonic into Elmer Fudd's scalp with his fingers. That was soothing to watch. I'm often soothed by watching other people get rubbed. But that Bugs Bunny episode was an adaptation. Of a classical song. Rossini, I think. Didn't *The Barber of Seville* used to be an opera? And wasn't the opera based on a play? Thing is, who has a barbershop pole for a head?"

"Maybe it's a fashion statement," said Mz. Veneklausen.

"Maybe it's a bunch of lizard shit," said Mrs. MacVengeance. "I mean, is Blankety Blank a robot or a man? If he's a robot, does he work for the government? If he's a man, does he work for the government? What's the government got against Quiggle Estates? Why can't the government mind its own business?"

Mrs. Flintlock added, "What's interesting is Blankety Blank has no motive. I heard on the news there aren't any links between the murders. Unless total randomness is a link. Like the police commissioner said, the murders were so random that there had to be a connection between them, a very clear and precise connection. Absolute order in total disorder or something like that. Pretty scary, if you ask me."

"Relax," said Mr. Flintlock. "We know you're scared already. You told us a hundred times already. It's probably nothing. He's probably nothing."

"Does it matter?" responded Mrs. Flintlock. "Something, nothing. Who gives a Sartre?" Except for the Zeelands and the Gamehater, the Erwin's guests slurred their words and teeter-tottered on their feet now. They wouldn't last much longer.

The Smiths returned from the far end of the yard. The Flintlocks, Lou Diamond Phillips and Connie Veneklausen followed in their steps.

"Sausages?" chirped Mr. Erwin.

Mr. Smith said, "Two lumps please," and got what he asked for. Mrs. Smith opened another beer and said to the Gamehater, "So is Blankety Blank a copycat killer? Is that what you're saying?"

Happy to be reintroduced into the conversation, the Gamehater replied, "No, no. Mr. Blankety Blank isn't a copycat. None of the murders he committed are full-fledged reenactments. Certain elements of each murder, of course, coincide with elements from other murders performed by other serial killers. But then again everything coincides with everything. For instance, I walked down the street today in such a way that was no doubt extremely similar to the way in which somebody before me must have walked down that street, and somebody before them, and somebody before them, and so forth, and so forth, and so forth, and so—" The Gamehater cut himself off with a loud squawk. "The point is, a man who eats his breakfast can be certain that another man the day before him has eaten a similar breakfast with similar utensils, similar rates of feeding, similar chewing and swallowing styles, similar degrees of satisfaction and dissatisfaction, and so forth, and so forth, a—" He clenched his teeth. "And so the key to unlocking the mystery of Mr. Blankety Blank does not reside in whether or not he is a copycat, because we're all copycats, and in the absence of copycatting, we would be meaningless."

An acerbic expression punctuated Mrs. Smith's face. "That's the last time I ask you a question."

Mrs. Erwin returned from inside the house, got another beer, and staggered towards her husband. "Children're ok," she muttered. "Hey, anybody know what that Van Trout's up to? I can see his goddamn silo from a hundred miles away. Well, from three blocks away. I can see it from my front porch, for Chrissakes. Sticks out like a big old dick."

"I second that," said Mr. Smith.

"Third," harmonized the Zeelands. Mr. Zeeland said, "Rutger's putting something else up, too. We passed his house on our way over and there were a bunch of construction workers playing instruments in the front yard. Not sure what they're building. But they carry a decent tune." He looked at his wife's chest, then at his own, comparing them. He decided his chest was inadequate and he needed to go to the gym. "We're leaving. Come on, Frieda." He took her by the wrist. "Thanks for nothing, Ingleby."

The Zeelands ran away in a hail of sausages.

"Where are the Van Trouts anyway?" asked Mz. Veneklausen.

Mr. Erwin said, "We invited them. They didn't come. They didn't want to come, is all. End of story." He chopped a sausage in half.

"I have to take another piss." Mr. Smith didn't bother to go to the far end of the yard. Nor did his wife.

Job MacVengeance woke up.

"What the hell?" he groaned, and dodged his wife when she tried to knock him cold again.

"More curious than the identity of Jack the Ripper," the Gamehater ruminated, "is the vehemence with which many Ripperologists pick a suspect and insist beyond a reasonable doubt that he is the perpetrator. Consider, if you will, the subtitles *Case Closed, The Final Verdict, The Final Solution, The Mystery Solved, Summing Up and Verdict, James Maybrick Was Jack the Ripper, Sir William Gull Was Jack the Ripper, The Elephant Man Was Jack the Ripper—Duh!, The Ghost of William Wordsworth as Ripper*...Granted, these and other subtitles were devised for purposes of marketing. Readers pay for concrete answers, however false, far more than they pay for admitted speculation. But one can't help question the authors' potential ideologies. Why insist Jack the Ripper is this Joe or that John without question? Because, like the existence of God, his identity will *never* be revealed, not in this life, and so, given the proper manipulation of fact, fiction and douchebaggery, the Ripper could be anyone. Could be me. I could be hundreds of years old—"

"I have to take another piss!" Mr. Smith shouted, still urinating. But he quashed the Gamehater's monologue.

Sound of thunder. Distant flashes of lightning. Rolling fields of clouds.

"Storm's brewing," said Mr. Phillips. He zipped up his jeans.

Mr. Erwin looked at the sky.

Mrs. Flintlock lit her thirty-fourth cigarette of the afternoon. "I'm drunk," she hiccupped.

Mz. Veneklausen parlayed, "I'm lonely. All I want is a good man." She ogled the men one by one.

"I'm a good man," announced Mr. MacVengeance, who had climbed up a tree. His wife stood beneath the tree, chopping it down with a pole axe.

Mr. and Mrs. Smith began to make out. So did Mr. and Mrs. Adrian.

Mr. and Mrs. Flintlock looked at each other uncomfortably.

Mr. Phillips hung his head.

"Heck of a day, isn't it?" said Mr. Erwin to his wife. She fell into a flower garden.

Overhead the clouds opened like stage curtains and it began to rain sausages.

———

Reluctantly the parents waited for them to recover, leaning against walls or bracing themselves on knees to keep from falling over drunk.

When the children did recover, all of the parents had lost consciousness.

The children poked them, tentatively, yet with a degree of assertiveness, as if the parents were jellyfish washed onto a beach who may or may not be alive, whose stingers may or may not be impotent. Nobody cried. And when the parents opened their eyes, the children hugged them, but not too hard, and not too desperately, learning from an early age, males and females alike, that manhood was just around the corner, a stinger's breadth away.

All Events Take Place in Real Time

Rutger Van Trout thought: There's not enough conflict in my life. I need some damned conflict.

He turned on the TV.

"The War Against Being Mean is forty-eight years old as of today. To celebrate its birthday, the President has ordered a surprise nuking of New Nigeria Twelve. Every time we nuke it, it just keeps coming back, but in the words of the President, 'Killin' feels G-U-D.' Additionally, the National Bureau of Wherewithal, in an attempt to silence critics of the war, has declared that all cemeteries in African and Eurasian Bluto zones be razed from bottom to top with exhumation canons. 'That way,' NBW spokesman Archibald Scalp proclaimed at the war's birthday party in Cleveland this morning, 'at least we know we're hitting something and can rack up a respectable body count.' Unmitigated genuflecting and cheers of hallelujah ensued. In other news, a serial killer..."

Feeling better, Rutger turned off the TV. He looked around. "Where the hell is everybody?" No answer. He ran the tip of his tongue back and forth across his hard palate.

He turned the TV back on. Listening to a short, speculative biography of Mr. Blankety Blank, he thought: When's the last time I had sex with my wife? Had to be over a month ago. Usually Francisco reminded him if he fell behind on his husbandly duties. Not recently, though. She had grown distant. Unsettled. Was she having an affair? If so, was it the first one? Maybe his wife had been having affairs for years. With who? Rutger couldn't think of any likely candidates. Maybe he was overreacting. It wouldn't be the first time. And nothing is as dangerous as jealously except religion and blind faith in a meaningful cause...How long had they been married? Rutger counted backwards...and tabulated fifteen years, give or take. Long time. Anything could have happened in that span. Rutger had never cheated on Francisco save the odd lap dance. Was Francisco getting lap dances? He shuddered at the image of a tanned, waxed, mustachioed Chippendale dancer rubbing his preternatural bulge in her face...He wondered what the Chippendale dancer did during the daytime. Nurse hangovers? Did he drink or do drugs before going on stage? Or was he one of those *toewijzings* who perceived stripping as an art form that must be approached with absolute sobriety, resolve, and social gravity? Did he even like girls? Most male strippers were gay, right? Did he engage in anal congress with the other dancers backstage before emerging into the limelight? Was it like a big orgy back there? What kind of man partakes in orgies on a regular basis? Rutger had never been in an orgy. He didn't really want to be in one either. Too much work. At every turn he would have to make the same throaty noises, the same contorted, percolating faces. And what would happen in the sordid aftermath of ejaculation? He would have to go stand in the corner or something and wait for everybody else to finish, trying his best not to look uncomfortable and flaccid...Did the Chippendale dancer own a suit? If so, did he take it to the cleaners or did he wash and iron it himself? If the former was the case, did he use starch? If the latter was the case, did he enjoy ironing, or did he perceive ironing as one of life's infinite necessary evils? Did evil actually exist or was it a social construction, uncanny or otherwise?...Has the Chippendale dancer ever used the word *uncanny* in casual conversation? In serious conversation? Did he have serious conversations? What constitutes a serious conversation? Resolute eye contact. Understanding nods. Taut jaws. Swabbing of the brow with a handkerchief. Evenly articulated dialogue about issues including politics, death, architecture, politics, and politics...Did the Chippendale dancer even know what *uncanny* meant?

"Where the hell is everybody?" Rutger repeated. It was 1:30 p.m.

———

At 1:31 p.m., Dr. Mark Tenbrook scowled at his latest Gamehater costume, a pastiche of galvanized Christian Dior legwarmers and Helmut Lang umbrella textile with an upside-down, cracked-in-half ace of spades cross-stitched into the chest. Nice-looking digs, he thought. His finest creation. But the cat had shit on it. He put the costume in the washing machine, poured in a double dose of detergent, and set the timer for forty minutes.

Mark ran two stories up a spiral staircase and emerged into an empty living room. Dizzy, he sat on the edge of an ottoman. Crow's feet marked his eye corners. His neatly trimmed mustache twitched. He ran a hand through an equally neat Beaumont hairdo and clutched a small paunch. Dark flashbulbs popped onto his field of vision and he thought: I'm dying. I'm dying now...No, it's just vertigo. But what if I were dying? I might be. I'm only 45. Too young, too young...I need bones. I need to crack a spine. Or at least phrenologize a skull...He stood...and went blind. He staggered across the living room, tripping over a series of meticulously arranged Japanese coffee tables. Fear took hold, but only because he might fall down. He had gone blind before...once. The first time he smoked a spliff. The only time. He was in chiropractic school. During the mock cracking of a crash test dummy's neck, "English Joe" Ackerman passed him the spliff and told him to hit it. Mark thought it was just an ordinary rollie. He took a puff and everything seemed fine. He pushed out his lips. He started to whistle. Then he couldn't see...Slowly his vision came back to him. He knew it would. It discouraged him, though. Drugs made him go blind once. Now running up the stairs blinded him...He cried out as the sharp edge of a coffee table dug into his tibia. It felt like the coffee table had bit him. He fell over...and landed on a chaise lounge...too perfectly. Nobody landed like that by chance. Was it an instance of divine intervention? Had a *deus ex machina* taken place within the strange womb of his McMansion?...On average he wondered about the afterlife thirty times a day to varying emotional extremes and critical perspectives. Now, reclined on the chaise like a model prepared for the flashbulb to pop, he wondered how old he might be in the afterlife. The same age as when he died? Or younger? Or older? Or would he exist in heaven or hell as an idealized image of himself? And would it be his idealized image, or whoever was in charge of heaven or hell? Or did some random *Frederson* make the call?...Deeds had to be taken into consideration. The accumulation of bad vs. good deeds—did they determine the state of his utopian post-self? More good, more utopian. More bad, more dystopian...Maybe everybody becomes stick figures. Black, featureless, long-limbed nonentities with no faces or genitals or phalanges. We'd walk around in the dirt and ignore each other. We'd silently contemplate the uncooked reality of having the same identity, of having no identity...permanent synchronicity, the death of Oedipal politics...Why couldn't Jung and Freud just get along? Mysticism vs. patriarchy, that's why...image of a staircase constructed from scoliotic spines...image of a wrestler piledriving an opponent...image of Freud dueling Jung in a cage match. Freud taunts the crowd, makes the Superfly Snuka sign, and leaps off the turnbuckle. He moonsaults Jung, then DDTs him, then nails him with a bicycle kick. He applies the claw. Blood streams down Jung's screaming face and congeals in his white beard. A red censorship **X** superimposes the scene, blocking the view...

Mark stood, blinked. Blinked again. Chewed a fingernail.

Taking careful, diplomatic steps, he walked down a labyrinth of hallways to the master kitchen.

———

It turned 1:32 p.m.

Mr. Blankety Blank stood in the middle of the Vulgaria and thought about Freud's essay "Das Unheimliche" as he sized up the aesthetic of a *faux chateau*. Then he thought: Blankety blank blank blankety blankety blank blank blank blank blankety blankety blank blank blankety blank blankety blank blankety blank blank blankety blankety blank blankety blankety blankety blank blank blank blank blank blankety blank blankety blank blank blankety blankety blank blank blankety blankety blank blank blank blank blankety blankety blank blank blank blank blankety blankety blank blank blankety blank blankety blank blankety blank blank blankety blankety blank blankety blankety blankety blank blank blank blank blank blankety

blank blankety blank blank blankety blankety blank blank blankety blankety
blank blank blank blank blankety blankety blank blank blankety blank blankety
blank blankety blank blank blankety blankety blank blankety blankety blankety
blank blank blank blank blank blankety blank blankety blank blank blankety blank
blankety blankety blank blank blank blank blankety blankety blank blank blankety
blank blankety blank blankety blank blank blankety blankety blank blankety
blankety blankety blank blank blank blank blank blankety blank blankety blank
blank blankety blankety blank blank blankety blankety blank blank blank blank
blankety blankety blank blank blankety blank blankety blank blankety blank blank
blankety blank blankety blankety blank blank blank blank blankety blankety blank
blank blankety blank blankety blank blankety blank blank blankety blankety blank
blankety blankety blankety blank blank blank blank blank blankety blank blankety
blank blank blankety blankety blank blank blankety blankety blank blank blank
blank blankety blankety blank blank blankety blank blankety blank blankety blank
blank blankety blank blankety blankety blank blank blank blank blankety blankety
blank blank blankety blank blankety blank blankety blank blank blankety blankety
blank blankety blankety blankety blank blank blank blank blank blankety blank
blankety blank blank blankety blankety blank blank blankety blankety blank blank
blank blank blankety blankety blank blank blankety blank blankety blank blankety
blank blank blankety blank blankety blankety blank blank blank blank blankety
blankety blank blank blankety blank blankety blank blankety blank blank blankety
blankety blank blankety blankety blankety blank blank blank blank blank blankety
blank blankety blank blank blankety blankety blank blank blankety blankety
blank blank blank blank blankety blankety blank blank blankety blank blankety
blank blankety blank blank blankety blank blank blankety blank blankety blank
blankety blank blank blankety blankety blank blankety blankety blankety blank
blank blank blank blank blankety blank blankety blank blank blankety blankety
blank blank blankety blankety blank blank blank blank blankety blankety blank
blank blankety blank blankety blank blankety blank blank blankety blank blankety
blankety blank blank blank blank blankety blankety blank blank blankety blank
blankety blank blankety blank blank blankety blankety blank blankety blankety
blankety blank blank blank blank blank blankety blank blankety blank blank

99

blankety blankety blank blank blankety blankety blank blank blank blank blankety blankety blank blank blankety blank blankety blank blankety blank blank blankety blank blankety blankety blank blank blank blank blankety blankety blank blank blankety blank blankety blank blankety blank blank blankety blankety...

———

(the) uncanny ([thē] ŭn-kăn'ē)

1. In a state of supernatural ardor. To be supernatural. Extraordinary. Beyond reality. Events or conditions with no logical or scientific basis. Colloquialism: "Uncanny as a shithouse rat."
2. Fear of the unfamiliar.
3. A term Sigmund Freud associates with the Sandman (nightmare-going villain) and houses (people-going edifices). Indicates a category of frightening objects and auras that initially appear foreign but ultimately reek of familiarity. Extrapolated from Ernst Jenscht's study. Marks the "return of the repressed" and, like much Freudian phenomena, effervesces with homosexual energy and *joie de vivre*.
4. Quality of life distinguished by untraditional behavior, puerile clowning around, and impulsive hogcalling that has been attributed to strychnine addiction and Irish genetic codes.
5. A novel by Paul Jennings and a book-length analysis by Nicholas Royle.
6. A subgenre of fantastic fiction defined by Tzvetan Todorov in *The Fantastic: A Structural Approach to a Literary Genre*.
7. In German, *Das Unheimliche*.
8. The opposite of canny.

———

1:34 p.m.

Mark strode into the kitchen, a vast expanse of laminate woodwork distinguished by monstrous gunmetal appliances, cavalcades of plasma screens, and an archipelago of cutting board islands and cooking ranges. Festooned in an Archdeacon apron, his wife stood behind Molokai, dicing vegetables and trimming chicken fat. He called out to her. But the space operas running on the TVs were too loud.

Sighing, he walked across the kitchen.

Two minutes later: "Can you turn down the TVs pl—!"

"Off!" yelled Pauline without looking at him. Dead silence except for the sound of a knife fluttering against the cutting block.

She looked good for her age, especially considering an unflinching lack of exercise. Her physique was naturally athletic and toned. She had healthy-looking olive skin and botanically enriched hair. Her breasts were fake, compliments of her second husband's wedding ring, which she pawned for an enhancement. Mark wasn't a breast man. But he couldn't deny a heavy-duty admiration for his wife's more-real-than-real assets. Her only potentially unattractive physical features were the wrinkles and bags that defined her dull brown eyes. In terms of looks, she dominated him. It wasn't the only way she dominated him.

A streak of dried mascara sullied her cheek. Had she been crying? Should he ask her if she had been crying? Should he ignore it? He never knew what to do. Typically he ignored seemingly out-of-the-ordinary incidents, whether they occurred on his wife's face or anywhere else.

"Smells good in here," said Mark. "What're you cooking?"

"I'm not cooking anything. I'm cutting." She stopped cutting and stared pointedly at Mark. It made him nervous. He couldn't think of anything to say.

"Do you know what the word *canny* means?" he blurted, then frowned, mentally tracking the origin of the question in his chain of thought.

Pauline said, "Canny? What kind of question is that?"

Mark couldn't decipher where the question came from. He couldn't think of anything else to say either. "It's a question." He wondered what it would be like to have nothing to say, ever, that didn't have something to do with the word *canny*. "It's a question," he repeated. He stopped himself from committing more repetitions.

"Jesus, I don't know," Pauline huffed. She took up the knife again. "Canny.

Something to do with cans. Like a room with a bunch of cans sitting around in it. Like if I took all of the canned goods out of the cupboards and scattered them across the kitchen. It'd be a canny room."

Mark touched the cutting board. "Would you like to have sex with me?"

———

"Sex?" said Francisco at 1:34 p.m.

Rutger nodded gravely. Confused, Francisco mimicked the nod. Rutger took her by the elbow and made a surprised, satisfied face. "Your elbow is smooth," he remarked. "I can't recall a time when it's been smoother. Frankly I can't recall a smoother elbow. Have you been using a new lotion?"

Francisco stared at him. "Is this your idea of seduction?"

Rutger contemplated the question.

"Look, I've got to make this casserole," said Francisco. "My skeleton's ghost is getting antsy. Anytime it's going to haunt me. And it doesn't know how to cook."

"Uitroep," mumbled Rutger. He let go of her elbow and left the kitchen. He cursed himself for marrying somebody whose parents named her after a city. Who names their daughter after a city? Especially a city that's so damned expensive. Costs money to walk down the street in that hellhole…

———

On her way out of the kitchen, Pauline changed her mind. She couldn't believe she had considered the prospect in the first place. "No," she said. She turned and faced her husband.

Mark's grinchlike grin became a tight line. "No?"

"No means no. Quit hassling me or I'll shout rape." She skirted him and started the long journey back to Molokai.

"But," said Mark, watching her. It was all he said.

Two minutes later, as Pauline squirmed back into the Archdeacon apron:

"You don't ask your wife if she wants to have sex! You just do it!"

The big hand on a gigantic stainless steel clock clunked onto the 8.

Mark left the kitchen ruing his marriage to a multiple divorcé, a perpetual malcontent, and a hopelessly Dutch wife.

———

dutch wife (dŭch wīf)

1. A long body-pillow.
2. A heterosexual prostitute or homosexual gigolo.
3. A fuck doll.
4. A hot water bottle.
5. A small wicker cage used to improve air circulation in hot bedrooms on humid summer nights. Sometimes used to enslave pygmies and opossums. Of Japanese origin. Also known as a Chikufujin.
6. A 👤 with ancestral ties to the Netherlands who marries somebody.

———

Mr. Blankety Blank snapped out of it.

The barbershop pole that was his head unfroze and began to spin again. So did his watch, which had stopped at 1:32 p.m.

He tore his gaze from the McMansion.

He flowed across the asphalt and Astroturf, through the Gazebos and Arc de Triumphs, over the rooftops and chimneyscapes and turretopias of the Vulgaria, hypnotizing onlookers that stared at him for too long. At last he leapt off of the Onderdonk's infamous turret, his body a tiny black Rorschach stain set against the blue vastness...he soared to the end of the street and disappeared into Ronald Conklin's six-car garage.

By 1:40 p.m., he had procured three fresh heads.

———

1:35 p.m.

Rutger would try again. That's what he'd do.

He sucked in his gut and returned to the kitchen. It was a fine kitchen—a quarter acre of space, plenty of TVs, decked out in glinting state-of-the-art superfluities. But it could have been bigger, flashier. And they could have built more than one kitchen. Some of the neighbors had as many as four. Maybe that's why Francisco had been so irritable lately.

"I'm back," he said. Francicso stared at him.

1:36 p.m.

"I'm back," he said again.

1:37 p.m.

"Hey, I was thinking of upgrading the kitchen. What do you think about that? Think that's a good idea? Let's just go crazy."

1:38 p.m.

Rutger employed THE VOICE, that deep-seated, demonic, would-be playful tone he always hoped would lighten people up and put them at ease. But THE VOICE never failed to make people upset and put them on guard. "Have sex with me," he grumbled through an agitated grin. "Have sex with me. Have sex with me."

"Stop doing that," Francisco warned him. "You sound like Satan with a hernia."

He stopped grinning. He looked at the floor.

1:39 p.m.

He looked at his wife and tried one last time. "Please?" said THE VOICE.

1:40 p.m.

He slumped out of the kitchen, defeated.

His son appeared at the end of the hallway and scrambled towards him. "Can I go play at Etcetera's, Dad?"

Rutger gesticulated madly. "Etcetera!" he shouted, overpronouncing the boy's nickname. Instead of THE VOICE he now employed a high-pitched chipmunk falsetto. "Etcetera! Etcetera!"

Unable to read his father, Rutger Jr. thanked him uncertainly and scrambled away, back down the hallway, out the front door.

Rutger Sr. followed him.

He tramped across the front lawn in the dark shadow of his silo. He placed a hand on the silo. The hand gripped hard on its cool, smooth surface. He arched back his neck and squinted at the rounded summit. The vestiges of nimbus clouds timelapsed across the sky.

"Super Balls," he whispered.

Later that day, the dump trucks and cranes pulled in one after the other and poured their wares into the silo's belly. Rutger observed the process with pride and relish. Neighbors observed it with bewilderment and antipathy. Soon the air of Apple Hill Court reeked of polymer, polybutadiene and vulcanized sulfur. The smell left Rutger intoxicated.

But the feeling of intoxication wore off.

Rutger went back inside. He called the construction company that had erected the silo and asked if they would mind building a barn in his back yard. The company's secretary-at-arms said, "No problem, sir. We can build you a skyscraper if you like."

"No thank you," Rutger replied. "A barn will suffice. And, if possible, would you mind bringing over some hay and a cow, too?"

CAUSE & EFFEKT

The buildup of shrunken heads underneath Rutger Jr.'s bed was getting out of control. Only by means of strategically positioned stuffed animals and action figures could he keep them from rolling out into the open.

And yet he wanted more.

Etcetera seemed to have an endless supply. No matter where his father went on business—Africa, Oklahoma, Israel, Yoknapatawpha, it didn't matter—he returned with ample supplies of shrunken heads, more than enough to distribute to his son, his son's friends, or anybody in want or need of them. At least that's what Etcetera told Rutger Jr., who, in a fairly short span of time, had developed a kind of addiction to the heads. He couldn't explain it. The heads terrified him. But he was drawn to them, and the more he accumulated, the more they terrified him. And the more of them he wanted.

Only one thing frightened him as much as his collection of shrunken heads: Mr. Blankety Blank.

The serial killer was all anybody ever talked about at school. Blankety Blank this, Blankety Blank that. Even his teachers were enthralled. In lieu of practicing times tables, reading Judy Blume novels, finger painting, and studying atlases and bushmen, curriculum now focused almost exclusively on the history, methodology, and long term effects of serial killing. According to Pine Ridge Elementary School's administration, the fundamental reason for this shift in pedagogy was a simple matter of safety and goodwill; if a kid could properly empathize with and understand a serial killer, then he or she could psychologically prepare for the possibility of being killed by a serial killer. A supplementary reason was to teach students not to talk to strangers in costumes. Five days a week, Rutger Jr. had to look at pictures of mangled bodies, crime scenes, courtroom sketches, taunting letters to the police. He also had to take classes on human anatomy. Every day fresh corpses were brought into school and used in mock plays that reenacted famous slasher killings. The reenactment of Jack the Ripper's alleged fifth and final murder of prostitute Mary Kelly, whose innards were removed and piled next to her body along with flesh from her abdomen and thighs, garnered acclaim from local critics and ran for three weeks straight, including weekends. Starring mild-mannered fifth grade teacher Mr. Bradley Gort as the Ripper, the reproduction invariably received standing ovations from the half-soused adults that attended while children looked on in unspeakable horror. By the time the production ran its course, however, most children had become sufficiently desensitized and could at least watch it without crying or experiencing feelings of dread, anxiety and psychosis. Not Rutger Jr. For him, each viewing was a cruel nightmare.

Recesses had been cancelled, too. No time for playtime with a stranger on the loose.

Naturally Rutger Jr. was too young to realize that his rabid accumulation of shrunken heads was an unconscious effort to surrogate his fear of being murdered with something scarier. Conscious or unconscious, though, it wasn't working. Worse, the heads facilitated his fear of being murdered by Mr. Blankety Blank. And they made his room smell funny. Like burnt potpourri. He lay in bed at night pinching his nose and wondering what it would be like to die and whether or not heaven existed. He wanted to go to heaven. But, even at nine years old, he knew that it probably wasn't there, partly because heaven made no sense, partly because his father was utterly ambiguous on the matter. Sometimes Rutger Sr. assured Rutger Jr. of heaven's existence, saying, "Anybody who doesn't believe in heaven is a dumbshit. Do you want to be a dumbshit?" On other occasions, he contradicted himself. "Only dumbshits believe in heaven. After you die, that's it. What's the big deal?" But more thought-provoking than the prospect of an afterlife was the prospect of pain. Would it hurt more to be stabbed and disemboweled by a madman or to be eaten alive by a horde of ugly, reanimated little heads? Tough question. It was all too much for a boy his age, he thought. Boys shouldn't have to deal with that kind of stress. Not until they're at least in junior high school.

———

How to Make a Shrunken Head: A Process Essay

The first step is to cut off somebody's head, preferably with a hypersharp machete or samurai sword for the cleanest severance package, but a pair of industrial surgical shears will suffice, or a guillotine, or a chainsaw, even a remote controlled mechanical shark will do. Ripping the head off with one's bare hands in not recommended unless one is a Shaolin Kung Fu master skilled in the art of Wuxia Pian.

If the head is removed from a live body, wait for it to stop gasping, thinking, and, in rare cases, screaming.

Make an incision in the upper neck area and carefully remove all skin and flesh. Do what you will with the skull. The South American Jivaro, who enjoy shrinking the heads of their enemies, throw the skulls into riverbeds as a gift to their snake-gods. Other communities use them as makeshift bongos, sell them to black marketeers or Spencer's gift stores, or simply throw them into trash cans.

Desiccation is the heart of the shrinking process.

Boil the skin in plain, hot water for roughly half an hour, take it out, and drape it over a stick or clothesline to dry.

Turn the skin inside out and scrape off the remaining particles and clumps of flesh. Turn the skin right side out and sew together the incision in the neck as well as the victim's lips, eyelids, nostrils, and ear holes. Steal a fistful of rocks from a sauna and dump them into the skin, or *tsantsa*, as it is called at this juncture. Roll the rocks around until they cool off, dump them out, and repeat the process until the *tsantsa* has shrunk to a point where the rocks no longer fit inside.

Now the shrinking process is facilitated by hot sand. Pour the sand in and dump it out, pour it in and dump it out, etc., all the while rubbing the *tsantsa* with charcoal dust and molding it in such a way that it retains human features.

In the end, the *tsantsa* should be the size of a fist. Tie the neck shut with a string and adorn the final product with beads, jewelry, tattoos, and whatever accoutrements suit you. (NOTE: A similar process can be enacted with animal skin to create fake shrunken heads, which, for many enthusiasts, are a popular alternative to the initial beheading process. Such fakes are extremely difficult to detect and fetch equally high prices from museums and collectors.)

———

That afternoon, Etcetera called Rutger Jr. and said, "There's a new shipment."

Rutger Jr. darted out of his room in a puff of dust.

He scrambled down the stairs, saw his dad at the end of the hallway, and scrambled towards him.

"Can I go play at Etcetera's, Dad?"

Rutger Sr. gesticulated madly. "Etcetera!" he shouted, overpronouncing the boy's nickname in a high-pitched chipmunk falsetto. "Etcetera! Etcetera! Etcetera!"

Unable to read his father, Rutger Jr. said, "Thanks?" and scrambled away, back down the hallway, out the front door.

Rutger Sr. followed him.

———

Three days and eight shrunken heads later, a small orchestra of construction workers played Dixieland jazz in the Van Trout's front yard with saxophones, banjos, clarinets, trombones and string basses. The construction workers still wore overalls and boots, but they had strapped on rudimentary party hats.

Neighbors gathered in the streets and sidewalks and began to dance. Some waltzed. Some sambaed and discoed. Some closed their eyes and waved fingers over their heads.

Mr. Van Trout marched onto the scene from the back yard. He cursed. He disappeared into the garage, reappeared, and fired a shotgun in the air...one-two-three-four-five-six-seven-eight times. The construction workers choked on or dropped their instruments. The neighbors scattered.

Smoke from the shotgun hissed across the grass like fog on a morning battlefield.

The construction workers disposed of their instruments, replaced their party hats with hardhats, and scurried into formation. The foreman stepped out of rank and brandished his token cymbals. Mr. Van Trout loaded shells into the shotgun and aimed it at the foreman.

The foreman dropped the cymbals and put up his hands. Mr. Van Trout lowered the shotgun, strode over to him and said, "The barn looks good. I like that shade of red, and the woodwork in the loft is superb. How much do I owe you for the hay and the cow?"

"No charge, sir," replied the foreman. "Those items are on the house."

Mr. Van Trout raised an eyebrow. "On the house? You mean in the barn."

"Sir?"

Mr. Van Trout fired and refired the shotgun until every last construction worker piled into his respective pickup, dump, or retro-Benz truck and drove away.

———

Two barn doors swung open in a flare of sunlight and revealed the silhouette of a figure with slightly rounded shoulders, faintly visible love handles, vaguely bowed legs, and a somewhat oversized head. The figure stretched its arms, made a weird noise, and stepped into the barn.

It was Rutger Van Trout.

He closed the barn doors and flipped on a light switch.

The cow mooed and batted its eyelids uneasily as it adjusted to the light. It stood in the far corner of the barn tethered to a banister.

Rutger walked towards the cow, admiring the minimalist interior of the barn. Stainless steel troughs affixed to the walls. Ladders angling into the upper lofts. A few mechanically inclined pens and stalls. Neatly stacked hay bales. A dumb waiter...Other than these objects, the barn was empty. Rutger felt a sense of calm in that emptiness as he confronted the cow. He petted its head and scratched its neck. He knew cows were stupid. Perhaps one of the dumbest animals on earth. Yet he expected it to respond like a dog and acknowledge his friendly touch with a groan of satisfaction, or at least a wag of the tail.

The cow stared at him. It turned and stared at the wall.

Rutger climbed a ladder and sat on the edge of the highest loft in the barn. He dangled his legs over the edge. He swung his feet. He climbed down and tried to reorganize a stack of hay bales, but they were too heavy, and he only succeeded in inhaling a gust of ragweed pollen that made him sneeze uncontrollably.

He left a bucket of grain for the cow and locked the barn doors behind him.

———

Layke decided to give up sex for Lent. She called Jamie Veneklausen to tell her.

"But you're a virgin," said Jamie. "And you're not Catholic."

"Yakety yak," said Layke, and hung up. Jamie called her back. "Are you a lesbian?" she asked.

"Lesbian?" Layke replied.

"Yeah. My mom thinks you are. She thinks you make out with boys so much cuz you're really running away from your true feelings."

"What true feelings?"

"For girls. You really like girls."

"So if I, like, started making out with girls, I wouldn't do it as often as I make out with boys, and that'd be good, because then I'd be doing what I really wanted to do, and when people do what they really want to do, they do less of it, right?"

"Uhm...I dunno. Mom didn't say anything about that."

"Your mom needs to get laid. When's the last time she went out on a date anyhow?" Layke hung up.

Jamie called her back. "Why are you being so bitchy? I'm just telling you what my mom said."

"I know. What're you doing later?"

"Dunno. Nothing, I guess. Todd's supposed to call. I should probably do some homework. I'll probably just watch TV or listen to music. Maybe I'll look at some porn. There's nothing to do. I'm so bored. Jesus. I need to get a job. I need to start playing sports or join Girl Scouts. Something. I mean, am I just being a teenager or is this what life is really like?"

"You're just being a teenager," said Layke, and hung up. When Jamie called back she had already left her bedroom.

She paused outside her parents' bedroom.

Rutger kneeled on the floor with a certain dogged reverence. A cubic aquarium sat on a tea table in front of him. Above the aquarium, a 72" wall-screen revealed a vacillating flotilla of idyllic, picturesque landscapes. In the corners of the room birds chirped and water trickled to the tune of soft, synthesized concertos...Inside the aquarium, a praying mantis stared at Rutger. The insect didn't move, didn't twitch, didn't chirp—it was the epitome of petrified resolve. Rutger tried to emulate that resolve. He failed miserably, blinking, breathing, squinting, flexing his jaw, clenching his fists, scratching his elbows, cocking his head, repositioning his knees...

"Dad?" said Layke.

"Son of a bitch!" shouted Rutger. He rolled into a standing position. "Damn it, why can't I sit still?" He threw an awkward shadow-punch.

"Dad?" said Layke.

His frenzied expression disappeared. "Oh. Hi honey."

Layke ran across the bedroom. She dove onto the bed, somersaulted across the bed, and fell off the bed. She hit the wall. Rutger looked at her askance as she stood and dizzily climbed back onto the bed and lay on her stomach. She propped her head up with the bipod of her arms. "Hey Dad," she said, cross-eyed.

"Hello," Rutger said stiffly.

"Hey Dad. Why aren't we Catholic?"

"Catholic?" He brushed lint from his shirt. "I don't know, sweetheart. The same reason we're not Buddhist, I suppose. It's a regional thing."

"Regional thing?"

"Yeah, you know. Regions. Places. Different places practice different religions. You live in that place, you practice that religion."

"Why?"

"Well, basically, it's because people are retarded. Asians, they're Buddhists. You go further west and you run into a bunch of Hindus, who eventually become Muslims. Keep going and everybody's Christian—Catholic, then Protestant. Go further and you're full circle, back in the Land of the Smiling Fat Man."

"What if you go north or south?"

"Up north nobody believes in anything. That's called nihilism. In the north there's too much snow and it's too damned cold, and if that's all you have, then there's really nothing to believe in. Down south it's different. It's all screwed up down there. Everybody's poor. Mostly southern regions just believe what they're told to believe by the people who originally colonized them—Christians, mainly. Or they worship turds in the sky. Or they spend all of their time running away from jaguars and hippopotamuses, in which case they don't have time to think about anything. Do you know hippopotamuses can run up to 30 miles per hour on open terrain. 30 miles per hour! Hippopotamuses might as well be dinosaurs, for Chrissakes. Or is it hippopotami? Anyway, like I was saying, what religion you practice depends on where you live."

"We don't practice anything, though."

Rutger smiled. "We're not like the others."

"I want to be Catholic," said Layke. "I wanna go to CCD and be Catholic."

Rutger picked up the aquarium. "You can't be. You live in Grand Rapids. If you want to be anything, you have to be Christian Reformed."

"I know plenty of Catholics, Dad."

"I know you do. But none of them are Dutch, and if you ain't Dutch—"

"Yakety yak," said Layke, crawling under the covers to take a nap.

———

As Rutger Jr. finished shaving his eyebrows, somebody tapped on the door.

"'Tis some visitor tapping at your chamber door," said a monotone voice. "Only this—and nothing more."

He leapt backwards from the mirror, wiped the remnants of shaving cream from his forehead and temples, hid the razor and hand mirror, and jumped onto his bed. He grabbed a comic book and shoved his nose into it.

"Son?" said Rutger Sr. He stopped tapping and pushed open the door. Rutger Jr. glanced up from the comic book.

"Why are you out of breath?" Aquarium in hand, Rutger Sr. advanced across the bedroom and sat down next to Rutger Jr. "Were you exercising?"

Rutger Jr. shrugged.

Rutger Sr. knit his blond brow. "Something's different about you. Did you get a haircut? I don't remember anybody saying anything about a haircut." He fingered his chin introspectively.

Rutger Jr. said, "Do you want something, Dad?"

"I wonder if everybody's gotten a haircut but me." Rutger Sr. set the aquarium on the bedspread. "Check this out. Look at this thing. *Look* at it, I mean."

Rutger Jr. abandoned the comic book and turned onto his side. "I don't wanna stare at your bug, Dad."

"Bug?" Rutger Sr. gazed at the praying mantis with apologetic eyes. "It's brand new!" He put a hand on his son's shoulder. Rutger Jr. shook the hand off. Rutger Sr. said, "Do you know how long men have been challenging praying mantises...manti, I mean." He reflected on his words. "The praying mantis is a great challenge, you see. No other insect compares to it. Sure, people continue to spar with beetles, grasshoppers, ladybugs, cockroaches, even dragonflies. But it's not the same. Nothing compares to a standoff with a praying mantis. They're the Lords of Discipline. They're the Monsters of Immobility. And yet they're killers. They're cannibals. Some have even evolved into carnivores. You'll never be a real man unless you can look a praying mantis squarely in the eyes and dare that mantis to look away."

"Have you ever done it?" asked Rutger Jr.

Rutger Sr. blushed. "Er, no. Well, I've dared the mantis to look away. I've done that. But it's never actually happened." He lifted and pressed his nose against the aquarium. "But I'm trying. That's the thing. You need to try."

"I shaved my unibrow."

"Unibrow," Rutger echoed.

"Werewolves have unibrows. I think I'm a werewolf. So I shaved off the unibrow."

The praying mantis cocked its head. Rutger's pupils dilated as he widened his eyes.

"Werewolves. Slaves...Did you say slaves?"

"No. *Shaved...* Shaved!"

The aquarium sprung from Rutger Sr.'s grip. He chased it around the bedroom, fumbling at it with hands and fingers, trying to contain it, but the thing was alive now, alive in spite of the organism inside that continued to stand its ground, and then the aquarium fell, and it shattered, and the praying mantis, immediately aware of being free, tore across the floor like a string of flaming gunpowder and disappeared into a vent. Two minutes later the insect stood atop the silo and stretched its forelimbs into the sky.

"Uitroep!" exclaimed Rutger. He marveled at the shattered remains of the aquarium. He looked at his son. "Uitroep! What's the matter with you? We had that unibrow taken care of. Coots took care of it. You don't have a unibrow anymore. You never did, if you want to know the truth."

"Yes I did. Yes I did!" Rutger Jr. began to cry. Rutger Sr. let him.

He asked his son why he shaved his eyebrows. Rutger Jr. gave him the same old story. By degrees, however, the truth came out.

Troy Conklin called him a lycanthrope. Then he kicked his ass.

Rutger Sr. considered using THE VOICE to put his son at ease and make him laugh. But THE VOICE had never made him laugh in the past; it had only made him cry. So Rutger Sr. employed THE ANTI-VOICE, THE VOICE's doppelgänger, a soft, understanding, comforting, almost melodic alto that assured Rutger Jr. everything was going to be all right. It worked. Rutger Jr. stopped crying and hugged his father, who hugged him back, and when the hug was over, Rutger Sr. drew two provisional eyebrows onto his son's forehead with a magic marker, making sure not to draw a unibrow, but two normal-looking lines separated by a sizeable portion of blank space. Then he picked up and disposed of the broken aquarium, told his son to get some rest, and left.

On the way downstairs, Rutger Van Trout thought: *Good fences make good neighbors...*

———

Quote

"When a resolute young fellow steps up to the great bully, the world, and takes him boldly by the beard, he is often surprised to find it comes off in his hand, and that it was only tied on to scare away the timid adventurers."

—Ralph Waldo Emerson, Man of Letters

———

On the way out the door, Rutger Van Trout thought: It's because we fed him espresso as an infant. But he wouldn't drink mother's milk. He wouldn't even drink formula. All he wanted was espresso. The stronger, the darker—the better. At one point he was up to four lumps of sugar a cup. That isn't right. A real man doesn't sip coffee beverages in his infancy. A real man sucks on tits...

———

Statistic

While the practice is discouraged, some people breastfeed regularly for up to eight years without any additional form of sustenance other than breast milk. The longest recorded instance occurred in an Australian male, Gale "Lunatic Soup" MacQuarie, who breastfed for twenty-three years, stopping only after he moved away to college, and who, despite being in his forties now, still enjoys "returning to the source," as he has admitted in several television interviews. Extreme behavior of this fashion, of course, results in extreme effects, among them emaciation (esp. Sméagol syndrome), adult onset jaundice, weak bones, calcium-stained teeth, proportionate dwarfism, premature eye bags, various forms of neurological anarchy (e.g. Damn Ham disease, a condition in which the brain takes on the texture and succulence of a fully processed honey-baked ham), and a teeming throng of social and psychological disorders. It goes without saying that these effects can be exacerbated by poor diet and drug use on the part of the breast feeder. Nonetheless Public Health Service officials sill insist that breastfeeding is both an effective method of nourishment and an acceptable lifestyle for children up to two years of age, this despite the growing number of anti-breastfeeding religious communities who believe that milk is an historically unholy fluid. "Jesus didn't drink milk," writes Lawrence Sockman, head minister of NCPMOCH (New Church of the Poison Mind and Other Cow Haters), "he drank wine. And so we advocate refillable cabernet sauvignon breast implants during the third trimester of pregnancy. Certain brands of shiraz are acceptable as well, but under no circumstances, God willing, shall our concubines be subjected to merlot from the inside out..."

———

On the way up the Conklin's driveway, Rutger Van Trout tripped over a tree root that had burrowed into the concrete. Struggling to right himself, he fell into a maladroit cartwheel. The cartwheel became a somersault and concluded in a kind of rolling bowling pin motion. He twisted his ankle. But he didn't stay down. He popped up and hobbled towards the Conklin's front door.

He rang the doorbell. No answer. He pounded on the door and yelled, "What did I tell you, Conklin! One more time I said! Open this damned door! Conklin open the door you fuckin' dipshit!"

———

An Encyclopedia of Rage

The contents of the following encyclopedia of rage originated primarily in the twentieth century and might derive from, as German sociologist Georg Simmel claims in "The Metropolis and Mental Life," "the claim of the individual to preserve the autonomy and individuality of his existence in the face of overwhelming social forces, of historical heritage, of external culture, and of the technique of life." By no means is this encyclopedia exhaustive.

1. Air Rage – Violent, aggravated and/or unruly behavior perpetrated by the passengers or pilots on an aircraft.

2. Computer Rage – Extreme physiological response to a computer or computer-related product (e.g. a word processor or video game). Typically involves verbal and/or physical abuse of a computer screen.

3. Bunyan Rage – Also known as Mr. ED (Endomorphic Disorder). Occurs in short, usually heterosexual males (under 5'9" approx.) who wish they were taller and resent other males who are taller than them. (NOTE: Not to be confused with Bunion Rage, which occurs when one gets mad at a bone deformity that grows on one's foot.)

4. Next Door Neighbor Rage – Holocaustic reaction to aggressive deeds performed by a homeowner's neighbors and their offspring. Such deeds range from bullying to reclusiveness to poor taste in home landscaping and yard art.

5. Puppet Rage – Occurs when hand puppets come into vogue and are used as a means of communication by the majority of a community's populace.

6. Rink Rage – Innovative defense techniques practiced by roller skaters who are repeatedly harassed by their peers.

7. Road Rage – Violent, aggravated and/or unruly behavior perpetrated by the drivers of cars that often culminates in one or more road accidents.

8. Wrap Rage – Violent, aggravated and/or unruly behavior perpetrated by the recipient of a mailed good who has difficulty removing its packaging.

9. Trolley Rage – Feelings associated with being run over by a trolley and other mechanisms with steel wheels.

10. Zenith Rage – A general, difficult-to-define unsettledness that results from viewing too many sunsets and/or sunrises.

———

Troy opened the door.

Rutger grabbed him by the ear lobe, stepped inside the house, and slammed the door behind him. "Conklin!" He glanced around the foyer.

No reply.

He heard TV static...somewhere. He followed the sound of white noise, dragging Troy behind him by his ear.

Troy didn't struggle, didn't squeal. Didn't make a sound. He allowed himself to be manhandled.

Rutger dragged the boy down a long, tall, barren hallway. The lack of artwork, photographs, posters, plants, tapestries, candles, tableaus, clocks, *anything* on the walls reaffirmed his boiling hatred of the Conklins. No wonder Troy was such a brat. His parents had no taste. Not even bad taste.

Troy's ear started to tear, to bleed. Still he remained quiet and docile.

Rutger rounded a corner, snarling like a panther on the hunt. He saw a door at the end of the hallway. "I'm coming for you Conklin!" He stormed down the hallway...

...kicked open the door.

Sheba sat on the edge of her parents' bed watching TV static. The wall-screen was on full blast.

Rutger looked at Troy. Blood trickled down his neck. He let go of him. He told the TV to be quiet. He looked at Sheba. She continued to stare at the now empty wall-screen.

"Where's your father?" said Rutger.

No reply.

"Where's your father, young lady?" He stepped in front of the girl. He kneeled down.

Sheba's eyes were milk.

His hatred faded away. He stood and said, "Stay here, kids."

It took awhile. But he found them. All three of them.

Surprisingly there wasn't that much blood. Rutger wondered why. Each victim had been beheaded. Then each head had been sewed back onto a different body.

Ronald Conklin wore the head of his dog. Madge Conklin wore the head of her husband. Sheba wore the head of her master.

Rutger Van Trout thought: Cock-a-doodle-doo. Cock-a-doodle-doo. Etc.

———

After he got off of the phone with the police, Rutger called his construction company. "Gonna need a chicken coop over here," he said. "Don't forget the chickens and the roosters. Please remove all of the roosters' larynxes. No Chanticleer's allowed."

———

Etcetera was far more striking than Rutger Jr. He looked kind of like an eggplant. A good-looking eggplant. His dark skin had a purple tint to it, and his oblong head was too big for the delicate body that supported it. Kids picked on him at school for not being Dutch as much as for his appearance. Still, Rutger Jr. thought he looked cool. Like an action figure.

"I hope my dad doesn't embarrass me," he said.

"He might," replied Etcetera

Rutger Jr. looked at himself in a hand mirror. "Do you really think my eyebrows look ok?"

"They're not eyebrows," said Etcetera. "They're magic marker."

"I *know* what they are. So you think they look bad?"

Etcetera smacked his lips and continued to pluck hairs out of the stitches of a shrunken head.

"All my dad does is get mad," said Rutger Jr. "That's all he does. I don't think I've ever seen him happy. *Really* happy, I mean. I've seen him smile a few times when he drinks beer. He laughs sometimes. That's it, though."

"At least you know what your dad looks like," said Etcetera. "My dad's gone so much, I forget sometimes. I have to look at pictures."

"We don't keep pictures in the house. Just big paintings of Grand Rapids and the Netherlands. There's one painting of Gerald R. Ford. And drawings of pelicans and gooses and stuff."

"Geese."

Rutger Jr. went to the window. "I bet my dad's over at the Conklins right now. I bet he's giving Troy all kinds of ammo to beat my ass in tomorrow. I'm not afraid to stand up to him. I tried that before. He's too strong. We're the same size but he's stronger. There's nothing I can do. My dad's making things worse. He always makes things worse."

"At least he makes things."

"And that stupid silo. And the barn. Do you know there's a cow in that barn? What's he doing? He's turning this place into a farm. Who lives on a farm?"

"What's a cow?" asked Etcetera

The bedroom door opened. Rutger Sr. walked in.

Etcetera stashed the shrunken head underneath the bed. "Hey Mr. V.T."

"Hello Eliot. Time to go home." He smiled sympathetically at his son.

"But he just got here!" exclaimed Rutger Jr. "Why's he gotta go already? What'd you do? What'd Mr. Conklin say?"

"Not much," said his father. "The point is, there's fowl on the way." To prove this point, Rutger Sr. got down on his knees and clamored across the bedroom, clucking, pecking, flapping his elbows. The boys regarded him with equal measures of bewilderment and fear. When Rutger Sr. began to peck them, however, they giggled, and then they giggled harder, and harder, and harder. Soon they were laughing so hard they couldn't breathe.

Blankety Blank

"Ouch."

"Quit saying that."

"Ouch."

"It doesn't hurt. You're exaggerating."

"Ouch. That hurts."

"I'll give you something to say ouch about." Dr. Tenbrook flipped Mrs. Coots onto her side, threw her arm across her face, took a quick breath...and pushed down, sharply, repeatedly, as if performing CPR on a donkey. Each push produced a loud crack of bones.

"Ouch! Ouch! Ouch! Ouch!" said Mrs. Coots.

Two rows of teeth appeared below Dr. Tenbrook's mustache. "There we go. Cause and effect. Works every time." He flipped her back onto her stomach. She said, "I can't take it anymore. You're no chiropractor. You're an animal."

"No. I'm neither. I'm a bone manipulator." His fingers walked up and down her back searching for knots and precarious bone formations. Mrs. Coots' slightly lordotic spine reminded him of a Ripper victim he had been studying recently, Ming-Lei Hoynsing. While not one of the Fab Five, in recent years Ripperologists had attributed her murder to the serial killer, namely Ripperologists who believed Jack the Ripper was an Asian transvestite who worked simultaneously as a geisha and a Japanese ambassador to England. He operated under a virtual legion of pseudonyms. Most popular was Frederick (or, as it were, Frieda) C'lom. Unlike many Ripper suspects, his motive for killing stemmed not from a moral objection to prostitution, but from being rejected by Whitechapel's ruling gang of prostitutes, the Yum Yum Cankers. Gang leader Mary Ann Nichols (a.k.a. Mommy Politique or "Polly"), the Ripper's first victim, adamantly opposed his presence in the London borough, and she coerced her girls as well as a number of high-ranking pimps to do likewise. Everybody knew C'lom had a penis, but he wouldn't admit it, and he kept passing off his asshole as a vagina. Eventually he was shunned and driven out of Whitechapel. For a short period he tried to focus exclusively on his ambassadorial duties. As his posthumously published diary *No Glot C'lom* indicated, however, he couldn't come to terms with banishment, and so he returned to Whitechapel to seek his revenge in the form of a Transylvanian ninja that loosely resembled a distinguished-looking British gentleman wearing a cape and top hat. Once C'lom started killing, he couldn't stop. In addition to Nichols, the Fab Five included Annie Chapman, Elizabeth Stride, Catherine Eddowes and Mary Jane Kelly. He eradicated them with increasing ultraviolence, then fled London and went on a worldwide killing spree. Hitching rides from stage coaches, rickshaws and pirate ships, C'lom traveled through the mean streets of eastern Europe, the deserts of the Arabian peninsula, the jungles of northern Africa, the icy vastness of Russia and China, the industrialized tropics of Japan...He left an international trail of blood and guts in his wake. C'lom died of prostate cancer at the age of 86 in Osaka after a ten year hiatus from death-dealing. According to his journal, the hiatus resulted from kimonophobia (fear of kimonos), which evolved into chronophobia (fear of time), and which culminated in phobophobia (fear of phobias). At any rate, Ming-Lei Hoynsing, his last victim, was the *magnum opus* of his homicidal library. C'lom skinned her alive, boiled and ate her skin while she watched, transplanted the stitched-together skins of three ostriches onto her body, glued a bill onto her mouth, plucked her, amputated her chin and cooked it on a grill, ate the chin, soaked her in a vat of warm cooking oil, and at last, when her body was tender enough, he sharpened his fingernails and ripped out her spine—the very spine that reminded Dr. Tenbrook of Mrs. Coots'.

Distinguished by an abnormally inward curvature of the vertebral column, the instance of lordosis wasn't diagnosed in Hoynsing until years after her death, when it became fashionable to exhume the corpses of murder victims, take samples of their DNA, clone them, insert them into different social contexts, and study what makes them vulnerable to killers. Hoynsing's aberration was discovered as an aside. Forensics experts and Ripperologists suspected lordosis resulted from the spine being ripped out of her body. But they concluded it was a natural formation. As Dr. Tenbrook ran his thumbs over the malformed thorns of Mrs. Coots' vertebrae, he wondered if her lordosis had occurred naturally. Perhaps she had been abused as a child, struck just so in the spine on a daily basis by an alcoholic father. It happened to Beethoven. It could happen to anybody.

"Were you abused as a child?" he asked, lifting an eyebrow. "Are you currently being abused by your husband?" Then, to himself, in an assured whisper: "This might be a job for the Gamehater."

Mrs. Coots looked over her shoulder. "What are you gibbering about?" she spat. "Monkeys gibber, not chiropractors."

"Bone manipulator."

"Whatever. Just rub my back and try not to kill me." She placed her face back into the padded donut hole of the chiropractic table.

Dr. Tenbrook said, "Let's see what's on the TV, shall we? Wall 4. On. BBC-GRIM."

The wall-screen dispensed a vintage blast of raucous, shushing pepper-salt that artfully faded into a breaking news story.

Merlin Version and wife/actress Steelie Magnolia had adopted another Nigerian baby from parents who wanted their offspring to have a better life. Now the Nigerians wanted the child back. Or they wanted a clone of their original child. Or an android patterned after the original. Or a stem cell, at least. Or money to buy some stem cells...The Nigerian couple told a newscaster in dilapidated French that they had been taken advantage of by the Aryan couple.

"Did you know Aryans originated in the oak forests of the Russian steppes?" said the newscaster in plain English. "Then they colonized Europe and established an empire in Persia. They spilled into India in 1,500 B.C., raping its indigenous peoples. In time they raped the entire world. The point is Aryans are Russians. Can you believe it?"

The Nigerians looked at him.

The newscaster looked at the camera, grinned, and signed off.

Hoping to start a conversation, Dr. Tenbrook said, "BBC-GRIM is my favorite news channel. What news channel do you watch?"

Mrs. Coots replied through an agreeable groan. "News is for eunuchs, Dr. Tenbrook. I have four children. You think I have time to watch the news?"

"You have time to get your bones manipulated," he mumbled.

"Pardon me?"

"Nothing."

"I heard what you said."

"I didn't say anything."

"You said something."

"I said two things: 'Nothing' and 'I didn't say anything.' Plus what I'm saying now, which makes three things I said now, and a lot more, if you equate each word I've said (and will say) with one 'thing'."

A string of drool fell from Mrs. Coots' lower lip onto a carpet tile.

"That was one week ago," the newscaster told the camera. "Today I'm here in Old Nigeria with Mr. and Mrs. Oopsayoohoo on the momentous occurrence of having their son delivered back to them. Emotions are mixed as the Version-Magnolia plane flies overhead and..."

The camera zoomed in to a close-up shot of the Oopsayoohoo's horrified faces as a whining black dot fell from the plane.

"Well," said Dr. Tenbrook, and grinded his knuckles into Mrs. Coots' coccyx. She screamed, squirmed, screamed, screamed...then passed out from the pain. Dr. Tenbrook crossed her arms behind her back, pinned them down with a knee, and rocked back and forth, back and forth, producing a fresh crinkle with each rocking motion. Runaway sighs of ecstasy escaped his lips.

———

A Short History of Chiropractics

Musculoskeletal historians usually locate the birth of chiropractics with late nineteenth century magnetic healer Daniel David Palmer, who, in 1895, declared that all health problems could be solved via spinal adjustments. This declaration was widely scorned by connoisseurs in the field. They begrudged Palmer for moonlighting as a beekeeper and grocery store owner. Nonetheless the die had been cast. By the early 1910s, chiropractic medical degrees were as commonplace as bowler hats, furniture factories, and people who believed that utopias were realizable modes of existence.

But chiropractics dates back considerably further than the turn of the twentieth century. It dates back to the earliest forms of intelligent civilization during a period of rampant Indo-European lycanthropic activity. Transformation to and from a werewolf wore heavily on the skeleton, especially transformation to human form, which, with some exceptions, does not possess the enhanced healing capacity of the animal form.

Following an epidemic called the Hundred Year Fur that involved a rare strain of airborne lycanthropy coinciding with an overabundance of full moons, chiropractors (originally called "bone manipulators") became valuable commodities. Pre-pharmaceutical subjects were in continuous need of back rubs and spinal adjustments. But there weren't enough chiropractors to satisfy consumer demand. Their prices rose to such a height that only aristocratic families could afford them. Before long, chiropractors were deified and worshiped as idols, and their services could only be accessed magically, if one prayed hard enough for their bones to slip back into joint.

Today chiropractics is alive and well, although practitioners are hardly the objects of desire and toadying that they used to be. Some detractors go so far as to argue that the profession is a hoax, equating the chiropractor with the Ripperologist. To have one's bones manipulated, they claim, does little for the patient except provide him with a temporary respite from back pain, which returns with a vengeance and forces the patient to revisit the chiropractor in a timely fashion. The more the patient is adjusted, the more his bones need adjusting. Hence the more pain he experiences. Chiropractics doesn't make people feel better, in other words, it makes them feel worse, and chiropractors manipulate bones for their own self-serving ends (i.e. financial gain) and peace of mind (i.e. the bald-faced thrill of manhandling a spine). A similar argument might be made for the Ripperologist. Contrary to the objective of his profession, this *poseur* doesn't really want to solve the case of Jack the Ripper. If he were to discover the true identity of the serial killer, his life would cease to harbor meaning and purpose, and he would find himself in a state of calamitous unemployment.

———

Graham Anvil changed his surname for a good reason: he had surgically reconstructed his head in the shape of an anvil. In some lights, he resembled the Elephant Man, or a hammerhead shark, but in a brutally handsome sort of way. Regarding him was like regarding a nouveau solar home or concept car—the architecture of his skull elicited feelings of wonderment rather than fear or disgust. In an age of increasingly competitive newscasting, Anvil had carved out a unique niche for himself.

"Good day, Vulgarians," said the newscaster in his token British monobaritone. The monobaritone had recently been upgraded so that its subliminal mantra—*love my head, love my head, love my head*—was now accessible to all commercial and most pirated sound systems. "Today we have a special guest, a very special guest indeed. I can scarcely contain my enthusiasm." He looked at the camera with existentialistic fanaticism, as if waiting patiently to be executed by a firing squad. "You know his name. You know his game. Sound off the clap-track for the man of the hour, the man with a plan, the man who might not be a man, Quiggle Estates most fearsome foe, the one, the only, the—"

"Blankety blank blank blankety blank blankety blankety blank blankety blank blank blank blankety blank!" boomed the clap-track. 3D television static exploded onto the set and engulfed Anvil.

As the static cleared, the camera zoomed out and exposed Anvil's guest.

They sat on either side of a small chess table in big disproportionate chairs. Anvil wore a bright yellow banana suit that may or may not have been dipped in oil. Mr. Blankety Blank wore his usual outfit—black knee-high boots, black overcoat with stiff collar, black stovepipe hat, barbershop pole head...The seats were so high, their feet didn't touch the floor. They looked like toddlers in highchairs waiting to go trick-or-treating.

"I'll start," said Graham Anvil. He moved a pawn two squares forward.

With a violent jerk of his arm, Mr. Blankety Blank knocked all of the pieces from the chess board. A rook nailed the camera, cracking it. The lens was instantly replaced.

Anvil screwed up his lips.

Dr. Tenbrook winced and clutched his forehead. It felt like the rook had struck him. He got dizzy and staggered backwards. "Deus ex Manipulator," he said. "Take over for me, please."

A panel in the ceiling slid open. Three mechanical hands reached down and resumed working on Mrs. Coots' back. She remained unconscious.

Chewing an aspirin, Dr. Tenbrook stepped towards the wall-screen and played with his mustache. Gooseflesh sprouted onto his forearms, his neck.

"The hand grips hard on the pavement," said Mr. Blankety Blank.

"Pavement almost rhymes with caveman," Anvil replied. "It's just a matter of three tiny letters. The replacement of the *p* with a *c*, the replacement of the second *e* with an *a*, and the elimination of the *t*. There you have it. It may as well be the same bloody word! Language is a mad scientist, sir. As for pavement, well, that's another story."

Mr. Blankety Blank tilted his head.

"I wonder how a hand could actually grip pavement," continued Anvil. "In my experience, pavement is a flat surface, and one doesn't tend to grip flat surfaces. One grips a baton. One grips a hairdryer or a sack of coins. But pavement? The street? You can't grip the street. Not in a soft manner, and certainly not, as you say, in a manner that is 'hard.' I wonder why you even mentioned it—the hand, the gripping, the pavement, everything. I hadn't asked you a stinking question yet. We were just sitting here and you blurted out this gobbledygook about an allegedly severed and sentient hand. People say things like that all the time, I suppose. Things that are unprompted and meaningless. Sometimes people say prompted, meaningful things as well. Whatever the case, I prefer the things that you say to be in response to the questions that I ask. Please, sir? It's my bloody talk show, you know, and I should be able to dictate the flow of conversation on my own bloody talk show. Don't you agree? All I ask is that you refrain from those kinds of outbursts in the future. Could you do that for me? *Will* you do that for me?" Flushed with rage, he didn't give Mr. Blankety Blank an opportunity to respond. "Fine then. Fine. I thought I'd begin our interview by asking if you have any questions for me." His red face faded to pale white. "Do you have any questions for me?"

Mr. Blankety Blank's upper half rotated from side to side as he appealed to the talk show's staff for help. Everybody shrugged.

"Uhm," said Mr. Blankety Blank after a long silence. "How long have you been a talk show host?"

"I'm happy you asked that question. It's a good question." Anvil put a small plate of olive oil and a long French baguette on the table. He broke off a piece of the baguette, dipped it in the olive oil, sniffed it, and placed it in his mouth. He chewed delicately, cautiously, eyes fixed on the ceiling. "It's decent bread. Not the best I've tasted, mind you. But not the worst. I like bread that's almost hard enough to cut the inside of my mouth open when I chew on it. This morsel is nearly there. Nearly." He broke off another piece and popped it into his mouth. He looked off camera. "Fucking hell. Can I get a sip of wine or something over here? You wankers expect me to eat this bread without something nice to drink? You're all fired, the lot of you."

A diminutive grip crept onscreen, put a small glass of red wine on the table, and scrambled offscreen.

Anvil sipped the wine. He swished it around his mouth.

He spit it out over his shoulder. "Disgusting. Now then. You asked me why I became a talk show host. Let's see..."

As he recounted the history of his rise to media mogul, Anvil ate the entire baguette, piece by piece. He also taste-tested and rejected five more glasses of wine. Thirty minutes later he said, "And here I am now, a scorching success and not a bad-looking cunt either, if I may say so." He smiled at the camera. Flashbulbs popped. His smile imploded and he regarded his guest with a grave, wanton expression.

Mr. Blankety Blank shifted uncomfortably in his seat.

"Right. Are there any additional questions then, Mr. Blankety Blank? I know you're a busy man. And yet you've donated a portion of your undoubtedly valuable time to my television show. Surely there's more you want to know about me. Or perhaps about my ideology? I believe in numerous things. I have ideas on a range of topics."

The serial killer raised a hand as if to cut the talk show host off and change the subject. As always, Anvil beat him to the punch. "It's no matter. I know what you're going to ask me. I'm something of a psychic, if I may say so. You were wondering what my thoughts are on the days of the week. More specifically, you were going to ask me: Why isn't every day Thursday? Brilliant. A perfectly valid question. A perfectly splendid question. Seven days of the week? That's ludicrous. That's altogether criminal. Every day should be the same day: *Thursday*. Think of the problems this simple reconfiguration of our calendar might solve. Weeks and months would cease to exist. And one wouldn't have to be late to appointments anymore. Are you continually making appointments on Monday or Tuesday that you can't keep? No worries, folks. The only day you will be able to make an appointment is on Thursday, and if you miss an appointment on Thursday, you can always make it the next day, or the next day, all of which are the original day on which you made the appointment that, for whatever reason, you were unable to keep."

————

Mrs. Coots' awoke halfway through Graham Anvil's soliloquy. She lifted her head and looked at the wall-screen. "What's this asshole's problem?"

"I know," replied Dr. Tenbrook. He had moved so close to the wall-screen that his nose almost touched it. "Mr. Blankety Blank is a strange bird. He doesn't follow the pattern of most serial killers. For instance, most serial killers don't go on talk shows until after they get caught. Some never go on talk shows at all."

"I meant the host."

"Don't misunderstand me," Dr. Tenbrook went on. "His acts of ultraviolence *appear* to be without motive—I'm not saying that's out of the ordinary, too. Historically serial killers' behavior often appears to be that way. Random and unmotivated. This isn't the case in pop cultural representations. Novels and films have almost always portrayed serial killers as beings who are *defined* by protocol. They achieve their identities as powerful life-takers, consciously or unconsciously, by dint of their killing strategies, their killing styles, and especially the sources of their motivations. Characteristically these sources manifest as paternal or avuncular figures who have sexually and psychologically abused them. In reality, sources are more difficult to trace, even with modern cognitive mapping equipment that allows us to visualize the mnemonic history of subjects. Mr. Blankety Blank seems to fall somewhere between a real serial killer and a literary or cinematic serial killer. His deeds beckon and invite codification. So does his media existence as an aspirant anti-superhero and a potential non-human. And yet the moment you begin codifying him, he resists it. And the more you try to codify him, the more he becomes utterly uncodifiable. It's like a trap. It's like a trap. It's like—" Dr. Tenbrook closed his eyes. His closed them tighter, tighter. He opened them, shook his head, and smiled. "One thing is certain about all serial killers, real and fictional. Their actions are rooted in identity crises. Most are white males under forty. And most of these males are produced by economic forces. Their killing sprees embody a quest for a masculine capitalist selfhood. Think about it. Serial killers really didn't flourish prior to the ages of industrialism and twentieth century capitalism. There was Indian cult leader Thug Behram who strangled nearly 1,000 people in the tenth century. There was French pedophile Gilles de Rais in the fifteenth century who raped and killed over 100 boys. In the early seventeenth century there was Hungarian sadist Elizabeth

Báthory who butchered as many as 600 girls. There was Jack, of course, and Dr. H. H. Holmes, and a few other harbingers in the nineteenth century. But not until the twentieth century did serial killing really take off and start to proliferate. The reason? A capitalist work ethic, and a failure to be a man and live up to that ethic. Period." Dr. Tenbrook's pupils dilated and contracted as he focused and refocused on Mr. Blankety Blank's glowing, swirling barbershop pole. He stood face to face with the image of the serial killer on the wall-screen. "He reminds me of some of serial killing's Great Gatsbys. With the exception of his head, he bears the most striking resemblance to the Ripper in terms of appearance. His conduct, however, invokes other icons. Gacy. DeSalvo. Lecter. Mickey and Mallory. Greenjeans. Hollerman...Blankety. Blankety Blank. Blankety blank blank blank blankety blank blankety blankety blankety blank...He's a fascinating specimen. One only wonders why he elected to run amok in Quiggle Estates. Is he from this place? Did he grow up here? Or will any Vulgaria do?"

Dr. Tenbrook fell into a philosophic silence.

Mrs. Coots didn't hear a word he said. She daydreamed about a trip she once took to South America as the chiropractor talked over Anvil's barbed voice.

Suddenly she snapped out of the daydream and realized Dr. Tenbrook wasn't massaging her. Deus ex Manipulator was. The machine unnerved her. She felt betrayed. She felt used, cheapened.

She screamed. She screamed. She screamed.

———

"The flamingo tells time by candlelight," interrupted Mr. Blankety Blank.

Graham Anvil stood up sharply, as if expecting the interruption. "This is not my beautiful house!" he intoned.

———

"You're doing it wrong," said Dr. Tenbrook.

"No I'm not," said Deus ex Manipulator.

"Yes you are."

"No I'm not."

"Stop saying that. I should know if a bone manipulation is properly executed. You're doing it wrong."

Mrs. Coots' continued to scream. Deus ex Manipulator muzzled her with one of its tentacles. Dr. Tenbrook said, "First rule of chiropractics: do not suffocate the patient." He reached underneath the table, pulled out a bokken, and hit the tentacle. Deus ex Manipulator hit him back, knocking him off his feet. He got up and leapt onto the renegade tentacle. He clung there. Deus ex Manipulator couldn't shake him off.

"This is unprofessional," scolded the machine.

During the struggle, Mrs. Coots escaped from the chiropractic chair. She made for the door. Dr. Tenbrook reached out and tried to stop her. "You're not fully adjusted," he said. Deus ex Manipulator agreed, then cracked like a whip and hurled Dr. Tenbrook into the wall-screen. Graham Anvil's voice skipped a beat. The voice sped up. It slowed down.

It melted into an electric drone.

"Don't forget about your co-payment!" exclaimed Dr. Tenbrook as the door slammed shut.

———

"Blankety blank," said Mr. Blankety Blank.

———

Scrabble, or, "The Blank Tile Is Worth Zero Points"

Doubtless the most intellectually exciting, challenging and dynamic of contemporary board games, Scrabble asks its players to form words using tiles containing individual letters. Each of these letters is worth a certain amount of points. **E**, for instance, is worth one point. So are **S** and **T**. **Q** and **Z**, conversely, are worth 10 points apiece—the most valuable letters in the game, but also the most difficult to employ in the words that players construct vertically and horizontally across the board. Unlike, say, the game of golf, the object of which is to accumulate the least number of points, the object in Scrabble is to accumulate the greatest number of points.

There is one caveat in Scrabble. If players prefer not to call it a caveat, they might call it an anomaly, or an irony, or a peccadillo.

There are blank tiles in Scrabble.

These tiles are chameleons in that they may function as any letter at any time a player sees fit to lay them down on the board. They come in handiest for players with small lexicons and/or limited word construction skills and strategies. Joyful sensations often accompany the deployment of blank tiles, especially in players who are merely proud of themselves for forming a full word. In order to prohibit these players from excelling in any way, Scrabble's creators implemented a safety device.

The blank tile is worth zero points.

——

Once he had secured Deus ex Manipulator back in the ceiling, Dr. Tenbrook turned off the wall-screen and called his wife on a phone-screen. Her expressionless face fizzed into view. She looked like she had been crying again. Bloodshot eyes. Red cheeks. And her eye bags were puffier and more wrinkled than usual. Or were her eyes always that way? Difficult to tell—for the first time in years, she hadn't put on mascara. He tried to remember if he had ever seen her without mascara on before.

"I want to come home," he said.

"You come home every day," she replied.

He placed a fingertip on the phone-screen. "Can't we all just...get along?"

"Black and white people get along. Husbands and wives—that's another story."

"But I love you."

"I know. I love you, too."

He smiled. She smiled.

She said, "I had an affair."

He said, "I know."

"I cheated on you with Lou Diamond Phillips."

"I know."

He nodded. She nodded.

He said, "I had an affair, too."

She said, "I know."

"I cheated on you with Lou Diamond Phillips, too."

"I know."

They smiled again, happy to have communicated with one another. It had been a long, long time.

Adulteration

"When you're finished, fax that report to the Hong Kong Collective," said Rutger to the BMW Futique. "Also fax copies of related proforma quotations, invoices, tax reports, meeting minutes, and whatever else you can think of. We want to cover all of our damned bases on this one."

The car said, "Faxes no longer exist, Mr. Van Trout. They're extinct. They've been extinct for, like, twenty years."

Rutger scowled at the KITT equalizer on the dashboard. "Machinery doesn't become extinct. It becomes outmoded, or outdated, or antiquated. Or obsolete, or old-fashioned. Or archaic. Or antediluvian. Or it just stops working and that's it. One day you'll learn."

Long pause. "At any rate, sir," whirred the car, "faxes don't exist anymore so I can't send one. Please specify an alternate method of transmission."

Rutger got out. He circled the BMW, opened its trunk, and removed a crowbar. He did another revolution. When he settled on a spot, he took a breath, wound up the crowbar, swung it down...and stopped before impact.

He looked at the car. He looked at the crowbar.

He put the crowbar back in the trunk, got back in the car, and drove home.

———

Parable

There was a man who wanted to be a monster truck. All day and night, he made vrooming noises and hurled himself over long rows of beat-up smart cars.

One night he welded giant wheels onto his elbows and knees...

"Whoever fights monster trucks should see to it that in the process she does not become a monster truck," said his wife when he tried to crawl into bed. She pointed at the door. The man fell forward onto his wheels and puttered down to the living room couch.

He dreamt of mud-stained windshields, Brobdingnagian engines and sperm whale spoilers...

The next morning, the man opened his chest and tuned up his arteries with a monkey wrench. He ate breakfast and drove to work. He drove over his secretary and officemates and finally his boss. He turned in his resignation and departed in an apocalypse of smoke and skid marks.

On his way home, he swerved into a lamppost and totaled himself...

———

Francisco was on the phone talking about Rutger Sr.'s father again. Periodically she called random acquaintances and explained to them what a weirdo Rutger Sr. Sr. was. This time she had verbally cornered Lou Diamond Phillips. She didn't know why. But it felt good.

"He was a shepherd," said Francisco.

"Shepherd?" said the old man. "What do you mean, a shepherd? Like a metaphorical shepherd?"

"What's a metaphorical shepherd?"

"I don't know. Somebody who takes care of flocks. A director, for instance. He takes care of actors."

"Do directors shave actors' asses for their wool?"

"Lotta shit goes down in the industry. I'm sure it's not unheard of."

Francisco smacked her lips. "Anyway, Rutger's dad wasn't a metaphorical shepherd or Alfred Hitchcock or whatever you're talking about. He was a *real* shepherd. He owned a bunch of sheep. Nutty bastard used to sit on the corner of Buttrick and 36th Street tending to them. Every day he'd sit there dressed up like a biblical Israelite—thobe, djellaba, press-on goatee, hubbly-bubbly pipe, and so on. Lunacy."

Since he answered the phone, Lou had been looking for a way to hang up smoothly and politely. He liked the Van Trouts and didn't want to hurt Francisco's feelings. But he couldn't help being intrigued. "Why'd he do that?" he asked.

"Because he liked to talk to people. The only reason people talked to him was to stop and ask what the heck he was doing. Didn't matter. He didn't care if people liked him or not as long as they'd lend him their lips and ears. And he told the dumbest stories and jokes. And he was always quoting people and saying sayings. Thought he was so wise. But he was just a pest. He was just a little bug."

"How did he make a living?"

"He was retired by then. He never made a living, though. He inherited a fortune from his dad, Rutger Sr. Sr. Sr., a self-made furniture tycoon who immigrated to Grand Rapids from Amsterdam as a child. Rutger Sr. Sr. Sr. carnegied his way to the top and built one of the world's largest manufacturing businesses from scratch. Rutger Sr. Sr. was his only child, so of course he turned out to be a loser. People whose parents give them things always turn out to be losers. The apple doesn't fall too blankety blank blank blank." She frowned. "What did I just say?"

"Blankety blank blank blank," said Lou. He added, "Say, I think I hear my doorbell. I've been waiting on a delivery of balloons all morning. Balloons make me happy and—"

"I have to go." Francisco signed off and retired to a bathroom to examine her throat in the mirror.

———

It was Wednesday. The kids had talked Francisco into letting them stay home from school.

For two hours, Rutger Jr. and Layke watched two children play Scrabble on TV. Then they practiced their gymnastics moves.

Layke was stronger than her brother, so she served as a foundation, knees bent upwards, hands in the air. Rutger Jr. straddled her and they clasped hands. Now the tricky part. He placed the arch of one foot on Layke's knee, inched it forward, inched it backward, inched it side to side. He quickly lifted the other foot and placed it on her other knee. They wobbled. They teetered. Rutger Jr. said, "Stay still," and Layke said, "I am still," and he said, "Nuh-uh," and she said, "Yuh-huh."

They stopped wobbling and teetering. Rutger Jr. evened out his breathing. When he felt confident enough, he pushed himself off of Layke's knees, hoping to accomplish a hand-to-handstand, but like before, he only succeeded in pushing himself 180 degrees up and over Layke with the grace of a quadriplegic…He slammed into the floor and lost his wind. His instincts told him to cry, but he was gasping, panting, huffing and puffing. Layke rolled onto her stomach and crawled on top of him. "Did that hurt?" She laughed. "It wasn't my fault. I was just laying there. You pushed too hard. Why do always push so hard?"

"Mom," Rutger Jr. wheezed…and a praying mantis galloped over his face. The insect trampled his eyeball, stinging it. He yelped.

Layke sprung onto her feet. The praying mantis veered towards a wine bar. She dove on it, missed it. She stood and dove on it again.

"Got it!"

Regaining his wind, Rutger Jr. crawled towards his sister.

The praying mantis escaped through a crack in Layke's tangled limbs.

They chased it through the McMansion for nearly an hour before the insect grew tired and allowed itself to be apprehended.

Layke opened her hands. The praying mantis stared at her. She stared back. Rutger Jr. stood shoulder-to-shoulder with her and did likewise.

"Think it's Dad's?" said Layke.

"Dunno. Maybe. Maybe not."

"That's helpful."

They stared at the praying mantis.

Layke said, "Should we give it back to Dad?"

"No," Rutger Jr. replied. "He's crazy with that thing. I think he wants to get married to it or something. But if he catches us with it we'll get in trouble."

The praying mantis stared at them.

"Maybe we should kill it," Layke said.

Rutger Jr. blinked. "Yeah. Maybe."

"Maybe we should torture it."

"Yeah. Maybe."

They stared at the praying mantis. Fifteen minutes later, they decided to lock it in an aerated Tupperware dish and put it in the refrigerator. They would have to think longer about what to do.

———

Le raisonnement

"Have you ever wondered why insects exist? It's not because they balance out the ecology, serving equally as predator and prey. It's not because God is interested in scaring people with little monsters. It's because insects teach us whether or not we're serial killers as children. If we torture and kill them, we might be serial killers. If we don't torture and kill them, we probably won't be serial killers. Ultimately, then, insects are decoding mechanisms by which we might test our psychological mettle in its developmental stages. The problem is, children who torture and kill insects often don't admit it to their parents. Why would they? If only we lived in a diegetic reality where children confided in their caretakers. Full disclosure is the cat's meow. A world without secrets, lies, dissemblers, cloak-and-dagger-lovers, emotional sneak-thieves and gamehaters..."

———

Rutger was going too fast when he pulled into the driveway. He screeched to a halt. Flare of red blips as the KITT equalizer schized.

"Sorry," he said.

He told the car to complete his work for the day. "Send out the rest of those telexes and make sure to file the confirmation receipts in your memory bank."

"Telexes are even more extinct than faxes, Mr. Van Trout. I don't think *telex* is even a word anymore."

"Something can't be more extinct than something else. Either it's extinct, or it's not. Just do what you're told."

He got out of the BMW Futique.

He surveyed the landscape of his yard.

He went into the chicken coop and fed the chickens and then went into the barn and fed the cow and rode up and down the dumb waiter and attacked a hay bale with a pitch fork and then climbed to the top of the silo and opened the manhole up there and stuck in his arm and fished around and pulled out a Super Ball. He sniffed it. He looked at his yard. He put the Super Ball back and climbed down the silo and chewed on his lower lip. The garage door was open. He didn't remember opening it. He asked the garage why it was open and it said, "Because I saw you coming. I always open when I see you coming. Why didn't you pull in?" Rutger retired to the basement of his McMansion. Dumbbells down there. He rolled up the sleeves of his salmon-colored Nautica dress shirt and told the dumbbells to set their weight at forty pounds apiece and picked them up and put them back down and told them to reset their weight at twenty pounds and picked them up and did one, two...three....four... ....five curls before getting tired and dropping the dumbbells on the basement floor. "Oof," went one of the dumbbells.

Rutger rubbed the flab of his biceps and thought: Once upon a time there was a kip-up...

———

Haiku

kip-ups make real men;
he leaps into the blue sky
& swallows the abyss.

———

Francisco watched TV as she fed dress shirts into a dry cleaner. The dry cleaner blipped and coughed as it processed each shirt, spit it out, ironed it with a smart arm, and put it on a hanger. The wall-screen played a local irreality TV show loosely based on Mr. Blankety Blank's killing spree. The protagonist dressed like the serial killer, except his overcoat was too puffy, and his stout, malformed barbershop pole looked more like a neatly graffitied fire hydrant than the real thing. He stood in an empty red room. Additional characters entered the room one at a time. They lacked faces; their features had been smoothed over with prosthetic flesh. They walked in languid circles as the protagonist sized them up and prepared to execute his token move, the GRIM-DDT, a rip-off of wrestler Jake "The Snake" Roberts' finishing maneuver in which Roberts falls backwards while holding his opponent in a front facelock, driving his head into the mat. Mr. Blankety Blank's maneuver had a small twist: before administering it, he cut off his opponent's head with a pair of giant garden shears. Effectively, then, the only things getting GRIM-DDTed were severed heads as the bodies they once belonged to loped around the room with blood and gore spurting from the fresh neck holes until they fell to the floor and petered out in decreasingly intense fits of twitching. Once the heads had been softened up by four or five GRIM-DDTs, the protagonist hurled them at a wall. They exploded like rotten pumpkins. Then he danced a little jig and a new faceless meat puppet entered the room.

Credits zipped down the wall-screen every minute or two. A disclaimer assured viewers that the actor playing Mr. Blankety Blank was the real Mr. Blankety Blank, who himself might be an actor playing a serial killer. Moreover, the barbershop pole head was played by the same pole that had recently won a Hackademy Award for its performance in a science fictionalized wall-screen version of Rossini's comic opera *Il Barbiere di Siviglia*. If Mr. Blankety Blank played himself, Francisco thought, his regular head-pole had been replaced with the Rossini head-pole, unless the latter belonged to the serial killer all along. Was Mr. Blankety Blank really an opera star? She wondered if he could hit low notes and high notes with the same efficacy.

Layke poked her head into the laundry room. "Hey Mom," she said. "Hey Mom. Hey Mom."

"I can hear you." The dry cleaner choked on a shirt. Francisco spanked it. That didn't work, so she picked up the machine and performed the Heimlich maneuver...The shirt spurted onto the wall like a ball of phlegm. Francisco put down the machine and shook her head.

"Gross," said Layke.

"What is it, honey?"

"Nothing. Dad's outside doing kip-ups. It's a contest. I think he might win."

———

Haiku (w/Alternate Ending)
kip-ups make real men;
he leaps into the blue sky
& makes a frog face.

———

He went to his front yard and lay flat on his back. He stared at the sky and inhaled the polybutadiene air. Soon he began to roll back onto his shoulders, slowly, so slowly that his movement could only be detected by the gravest scrutiny. But then it couldn't be denied: Rutger Van Trout was teetering back and forth like a see-saw, and when he teetered onto his shoulders, he paused for a moment, placing his hands aside his ears and gripping the Astroturf, preparing to spring onto his feet, to fling his legs upwards and kick them beneath his underside in one fluid motion, finally to plant his feet and explode into an erect position, and the more air he kept between his body and the Astroturf during the kip-up, the better...Just as he looked like he was about to spring, however, he rocked onto his bottom with a Sisyphuslike sigh. He still hadn't adequately psyched himself out. He needed to succeed on the first try. The third, the eighth, the twenty-first try wouldn't do—and yet if he failed on the first try, he would keep going despite himself.

A crowd of Vulgarians formed around the Dutchman. Neighbors, children, McMansion builders, dogwalkers, dogcatchers, truant officers, ice cream truck drivers, dandies and flâneurs...

The crowd placed bets on Mr. Van Trout. They bet on how long he would continue rocking before actually attempting a kip-up. They bet on how many tries it would take him to successfully accomplish a kip-up. They bet on the likelihood of Mr. Van Trout never successfully accomplishing a kip-up in lieu of giving up or tiring out.

At last, he entertained the maneuver. His legs shot upwards...and slammed into the Astroturf like the spring-loaded bar of a mousetrap. Spikes of pain attacked his calves, his thighs. He cursed until he was hoarse, yet he remained supine. Dirty wads of cash passed between the frantic hands of onlookers.

Mr. Van Trout stopped cursing and rocked onto his shoulders.

He got a little more air on the second try. But he still failed. This time his tailbone caught the brunt of the fall. He rolled onto his side and arched his back in agony. He croaked obscenities, wondering if he had landed on a rock. But there were no rocks in the Astroturf. It was a smooth, state-of-the-art, self-cleaning artificial lawn. Even the smallest pebble couldn't endure its surface for more than a few seconds before a mouth in the lawn opened, consumed and digested it.

More money. More bets. Some heckling.

Enraged, Mr. Van Trout commenced a long series of rapid kip-ups, none of which came to fruition. He looked like an overturned turtle having an epileptic seizure. His arms and legs and head gesticulated and flailed, but his back seemed to be fused to the ground. His bones creaked and crinkled. His blond hair frizzed into a scruffy mane. His face turned the color of a turnip. Still, he kept at it. He would die before he allowed himself not to do a kip-up. The kip-up became his enemy. He could only conquer his enemy by performing his enemy.

Dr. and Mrs. Tenbrook held hands as they passed by Mr. Van Trout's

McMansion. They stopped. Dr. Tenbrook had been expounding on the vicissitudes of modern day Ripperology while his wife simulated attentiveness and daydreamed about kitchenware. The spectacle of Mr. Van Trout's unlikely kip-up, however, interrupted their trains of thought.

They pushed their way to the front of the pack. "Look at that bastard," said the chiropractor. He shook his head. "Look at that bastard."

"You said it twice," said Mrs. Tenbrook.

"Said what twice?" asked Dr. Tenbrook.

She rumpled her lips. "Look at that bastard."

"I just said that." He rearranged his belt. "I can do that. I used to do those things all the time. I was a champion in high school. Kip-up Tenbrook, they called me."

"Apropos." Mrs. Tenbrook glared at her husband. "Ok. I'm leaving now." She walked away. Dr. Tenbrook, in turn, dove onto the Astroturf next to Mr. Van Trout and tried and failed to do a kip-up. He tried and failed again. Again. Again.

"Tenbrook, you son of a bitch!" huffed Mr. Van Trout, not missing a beat.

"Go Dad!" said Rutger Jr. The boy had just made the scene. So had Layke, returning with her mother to watch the two middle-aged warriors battle for glory.

———

Troy Conklin cleaned his suit with a lint brush, then looked in the mirror. He adjusted the nub of his tie. He smiled. He nodded. He stuck out his hand and simulated a handshake and smiled and nodded and smiled and nodded.

"Good morning, sir," he articulated.

"Good evening, ma'am," he articulated.

"What the devil have you done with the begonias, you pork sword?" he inquired.

Sheba entered the bedroom. She wore a suit coat and skirt and a pillbox hat. She said, "The early bird catches the worm."

Troy said, "The perceptive worm sleeps with the fishes."

On Worms

Before turning his attention to monkeys, British naturalist and agnostic Charles Darwin studied worms. He discovered that earthworms played a significant role in the formation of soil, and in 1837, he revealed his discovery to the Geological Society in the form of an academic essay that he read aloud, word for word, pausing only to clear his throat, sip water, and comb his sideburns. Afterwards certain members of the audience talked wildly about his speaking voice, claiming that it was "inspired" and "gripping." Others disagreed. One man, for instance, approached Darwin in the public lavatory and accused him of improperly using the word "frolic." Shaking himself dry, Darwin looked over his shoulder and replied, "Das Ausscheiden fühlt gut."

Darwin later wrote a book on worms called *The Formation of Vegetable Mould, through the Action of Worms, with Observations on their Habits*. The working title for this piece was *The Formation of Vegetable Mould, through the Action of Verms, with Observations on their Habits*. When he said the word worm aloud, Darwin enjoyed replacing the *w* with a *v*, and consequently the *o* with an *e* (for phonetics' sake), viz., verms. "It sounds better to me that way," he told his publisher, "and it's a lot more fun to say it that way." Hence the working title of the book, which Darwin wanted to be the final title, and every time he mentioned the word worms in the body of the text, he wanted it to be spelled his way. He went so far as to visit Noah Webster and request that the spelling of worms be altered in the dictionary. Nobody obliged him. Hence the shift in focus from worms to natural selection and evolution...

Eventually Darwin went bald and grew a beard down to his navel. He suffered from seasickness. He had heart palpitations. He vomited frequently and broke out in boils and cold shakes. He felt badly for the way Americans treated Indians. He missed his daughter Annie; like all of his children, she died of scarlet fever and trampled his faith in a Christian God. On his deathbed, Darwin converted back to Christianity, but he still believed in monkeys. "I'll always believe in monkeys," he said to his wife, and then slipped away.

———

Rutger Van Trout and Mark Tenbrook stared at the sky. The mob had dispersed. Everybody had dispersed.

During the mêlée, Rutger nearly fainted from a combination of fatigue and anxiety. So did Mark, who, for a split second, felt something welling up in him, something he hadn't felt since junior high school: a hate wave. The sensation dissipated before it had a chance to flourish, but its resurgence concerned him. What did it mean? Needless to say, neither competitor did a kip-up. Not even close.

Slowly they stopped panting. Their breathing grew steady, and they stood and faced each other, brothers in failure.

"All right, Tenbrook," said Rutger, dusting himself off. He stuck out his hand.

Mark shook it. "All right. So long."

"So long."

Massaging elbows and hips, the chiropractor limped away. Rutger watched him go.

Ronald Conklin's Volvo 9000 Swedespeed pulled into the driveway next door. The doors swooshed open, and Troy and Sheba stepped out. Their business clothes looked freshly cleaned and pressed.

Rutger narrowed his eyes. "What the heck?"

The doors of the Swedespeed obediently swooshed closed and the children made for the front door. Rutger called out to them. They froze, as if paused in a film. Rutger called out to them again. They remained frozen. Rutger walked into the Conklin's yard and up the driveway. "Kids?" No response. He reached down and placed a hand on Troy's shoulder. The boy tensed. "Troy?"

The boy turned around and faced his neighbor.

Rutger cocked his head. He took a step backwards and cocked his head in the other direction. Troy looked different. It wasn't his little suit either, although that was certainly peculiar. Something about his face. It didn't look plain anymore. It looked...the opposite of plain. What would that be? Striking.

Resonant. Distinctive and utterly singular. And yet Rutger couldn't put his finger on exactly what was striking, resonant, distinctive and utterly singular.

"Did you get a face lift?" he asked.

Troy batted his eyes. "Good morning, sir." He bowed deeply.

Rutger looked at Sheba. She hadn't turned around. He looked at Troy. "Isn't your aunt supposed to be staying with you?"

Troy bowed again. "Yes. Our aunt stayed with us. She stayed here." He turned and pointed at his house. "Then we told her to go home. We didn't need her. We don't need anybody. Everything is a lot easier now. Life is a cinch."

Rutger inhaled, exhaled. "Why aren't you at school?"

"School?" said Troy, befuddled. Sheba giggled. Troy said, "School is for sidewinders. We work. We go to work." Now he pointed at the Swedespeed.

"Uhm," said Rutger.

"Please excuse us, sir," intoned Troy. "We are having people over for a business luncheon and need to prepare the appetizers. You understand." He delivered another bow. "Good day." He pivoted on a heel and strode inside. Sheba followed him. Before disappearing into the house, Troy looked over his shoulder and said, "FYI tell Rutger Jr. I'm sorry. And tell him to keep his chin up. And tell him...Flimflam. Flimflam. I am the Egg Man."

"Uhm," said Rutger...

———

...and the palatial, stainless steel door of the refrigerator yawned open.

"Uitroep!"

Rutger removed the Tupperware dish. He opened it and stared at its contents.

The praying mantis rubbed its long hands together like a greedy cartoon villain.

Rutger Jr. and Layke burst into the kitchen in a clumsy somersault of tickling and laughter. When they saw their father, however, they quieted, settled, stood.

"Where'd this damned thing come from?" he asked them. "I thought I lost this damned thing."

"Dunno," said Rutger Jr. Out of the corner of her mouth, Layke whispered, "I guess we're giving it back to him."

To celebrate, Rutger Sr. cooked everybody a bowl of Hutspot with a side of Leidse cheese.

A Short History of Grand Rapids
Chapter 1

The first chapter of *The Story of Grand Rapids*, edited by Z. Z. Lydens, is called "The Where and the Why." "Grand Rapids is a city that had to be," writes Lydens. "Its name is indigenous. It derived from the rapids and the Indian name for the river, Owashtanong, the faraway waters, translated with a French accent into Grand."

The founder of Grand Rapids, Louis Campau (1791-1871), a fur trader, was publicly castigated by the Church for selling ten barrels of whiskey to a local tribe of Indians, whose squaws got drunk and tried to bite off each other's noses. The Church threatened to cut off Campau's nose if he sold liquor to the Indians again.

Campau first came to the Grand Rapids area in 1826. He wore a beret and carried a walking stick. He met some Indians and tried to communicate with them by way of sign language and simian grunts. The Indians looked at each other blankly and nicknamed Campau "Giiwanaadizi Wayaabishkiiwed," which, in their native tongue, means "Craaaaaaaaaaaaaazy White Man!" Frustrated, the Frenchman left, but he came back in 1827, this time with his wife Sophie de Masac. She, too, tried and failed to communicate with the Indians. Her efforts to communicate with the local Yankees were also foiled as she could only speak French.

Somehow Sophie managed to make a friend, one Mrs. Slater, the wife of a missionary, who she conversed with using various frowns, lip arrangements, nods, and jawbone flexes. [TEXT MISSING HERE]

The Indians were fascinated by Giiwanaadizi Wayaabishkiiwed's handlebar mustache. Sometimes they took hold of its ends and tugged on them like buffalo udders. Campau found the gesture laughable, even endearing, but over time it started to annoy him, and he considered shaving off the mustache. Sophie insisted he keep it, however, arguing that his identity was largely defined by the prowess of his facial hair. Campau agreed. And the next time an Indian reached out to milk his face, he disemboweled the Indian with his walking stick, putting an end to further acts of molestation.

———

A Short History of the Handlebar Mustache

Several famous personages have boasted this particular brand of facial hair at some point in their lives, among them Napoleon III, Joseph Stalin, Triple H, Gene Shalit, Kaiser Wilhelm II, King Arthur, Salvador Dali, Pontius Pilot, and Burt Reynolds. Some critics argue that Edgar Allen Poe repeatedly tried to grow handlebars, but his mustache refused to oblige him, unwilling to develop past the corners of his lips. Here is the impetus for the writer's notorious decline into alcoholism and self-pity.

According to Gene Shalit, the first handlebar mustache was grown by Maury Fichtenbaum (b. circa 493 B.C.), contemporary, friend, and ostensible ghost writer for Sophocles (b. circa 496 B.C.). Fichtenbaum got the idea from an actor on the set of *Oedipus Rex*. Hungry for his co-stars' attention, the actor kept putting a dead blackbird to his overlip and honking like a Model T. Fichtenbaum raised an eyebrow...and vanished for four months, leaving Sophocles to fend for himself. (During this period, ironically, the ancient Greek tragedian experienced a powerful surge of creativity and produced two one-acts on his own, *The Bovine Tracheas* and *Donkey Kong*. The first play was lost. The other was adapted into a video arcade game in 1981 by Shigeru Miyamoto.) When Fichtenbaum returned, Sophocles barely recognized him. The new mustache utterly bemused him and he mistook the old Hebrew for an evil twin. Sophocles stabbed him. Fichtenbaum survived. He even managed to convince Sophocles that he was in fact himself. But being stabbed changes a man...Shalit's claim has been discounted by most physiognomists, who argue that the late film and book critic was just trying to appear knowledgeable beyond his own intellectual resources. There's no reason, as they see it, why primitive *homo sapiens* as old as 250,000 years couldn't grow and nurture handlebar mustaches. Men have been shaving their facial hair into funny shapes for a long time, after all.

Since its inception, the handlebar mustache experienced ebbs and flows in popularity. The dawn of the twentieth century marked the beginning of its terminal decline. Nowadays it is relegated, for the most part, to circus folk, Bavarian mafia bosses, bikers, hunger artists, and actors who do period piece films. The virtual disappearance of the mustache has generally been attributed to capitalist forces. Why capitalism rejected it, however, is a source of great debate.

A Short History of Grand Rapids
Chapter 2

Beneath the mechanical, blipped, autogeddoned urban sprawl is a vision of nature in its purest form...When Louis Campau stood at the of the top of the valley that would become the groaning belly of Grand Rapids, he beheld wooded slopes, deep green thickets, ridges of clay, plateaus, bluffs, meadows, maple and cedar swamps, all of it penetrated by a rippling crystal river. The sound of rapids purred in the distance. The canvas of sky was overwhelming, too vast to comprehend. So much rolling space. At the sight of it, Campau felt short of breath, caught between feelings of euphoria and dread.

Girders and construction beams [TEXT MISSING HERE] a chain gang paved the length of Fulton Street, and Gaslight Village materialized almost overnight.

A share of Campau's countrymen followed him to Michigan. So did many other western Europeans (e.g. Irish, German, Polish, Scandinavian, Lithuanian, Italian, Greek, Syrian and Latvian peoples). No Aryan nation, however, was more prominently represented in the Grand Rapids area than the Netherlands. Dutch people were enthralled by Western Michigan. They possessed a special knack for making furniture, and here they had more trees at their disposal than in their wildest hashish-induced dreams. Thus Western Michigan became the center of Dutch immigration in the 19th century, and Grand Rapids became the frenzied pulse of Dutch American cosmopolitan life.

By the turn of the century, Grand Rapids was the United States' leading furniture manufacturing city. Riotously popular at this time was a specialty chair called the J. B. Wrongway. Conceptualized by the city's greatest promoter, industrialist John Ball, the chair had been constructed so that users could sit upside down, comfortably, without blood rushing to their heads. Wrongways became a totem of Grand Rapids' culture. One could be found in every bourgeois household. Many households only contained Wrongways. Entire dinner parties took place upside down. People got used to it—especially the Dutch—to the extent that sitting upright evolved into a marginalized phenomenon. During the 1910s, there was even a period when many Grand Rapidians could be seen upside down in public, either doing handstands or walking across the streets on their hands. All this died out in the 20s, though, and the Wrongway met a quick demise when it was posthumously discovered that John Ball had concocted the article of furniture not as an upper class novelty item and salon discussion piece but as the result of a bet he made with his brother Bill. "Five hundred dollars says I can turn this madcap city on its ass," said John. "Why? Because I says I can."

By no means did the death of the Wrongway mark the death of the furniture industry. The industry continued to flourish until the 1950s when two middle-aged Dutch American suburbanites began making biodegradable soap in their basements using test tubes, Bunsen burners, and Chemistry 101 textbooks. They knew the American Dream wouldn't arbitrarily go to bed with them. To live that dream, one had to chase and poach it actively, indefatigably, by force of will and desire. And when they sold their first bucket of soap, they traded knowing glances and simultaneously whispered to each other, "You ain't much if you ain't Dutch," which today exists as a tag line for their multibillion dollar corporate dynasty.

A Short History of the American Dream (Capitalist Illusion)

Coined by James Truslow Adams in *The Epics of America* (1931), the term hinges on the illusion that anybody can rise to the top of the American capitalist socioeconomic pyramid. If everybody rose to the top, however, there could be no bottom, no middle, and the system would collapse. It would fall out of the sky like a shrunken head somebody absently tossed out of a hot air balloon. Herein resides the "dream" element of the term.

A Short History of the Dream (Unconscious Experience)

...whereas in *The Interpretation of Dreams*, Freud equates it with psychosis, explaining that it is a wish-fulfillment fantasy. The dream is thus a state of hard-boiled insanity. But this is elementary psychoanalysis. Freud's true feelings surface in a footnote to the second chapter, "The Method of Interpreting Dreams: An Analysis of a Specimen Dream": "There is at least one spot in every dream at which it is unplumbable—a navel, as it were, that is its point of contact with the unknown" (143). Dream theorists debate whether or not Freud included this "observation" as a disclaimer for material he either didn't understand or didn't feel like thinking about in sufficient depth. If nothing else, they say, it was a way for him to justify putting down his pen to have a snack. He was a neurotic workaholic, and only when he believed something was genuinely, organically "unplumbable" could he tear himself away from it.

According to cave drawings, it is believed that Yen-shu Phrase (d.o.b. unknown), a Chinese barber, proto-human, and member of the Yicfung clan, experienced the first coherent dream. The dream was simple. A jar of baby pickles sat on a table. Phrase approached the jar, opened it, and swallowed every baby pickle whole...except one. This final pickle transformed into a tadpole, then a fish, then a frog, then a miniature dinosaur, then a miniature human being, at which point Phrase sealed the jar. The human being looked sadly at his captor before exploding like a moist firecracker.

Phrase awoke. Crabby and fatigued, he told his family and peers about his experience. They neither believed nor understood him. What was a dream? Nobody knew. Nobody had ever gotten anything less than a good night's sleep. But "The Last Pickle," as the dream was called, proved to be infectious, and in a very short time period, dreaming went global. Nobody slept soundly. Everybody tossed and turned and REMed. Yicfungians had nightmares and woke up screaming. They had wet dreams and ejaculated in their bedsheets. And when the tormented sleepers crawled out of bed, they were crabby and fatigued... Socioeconomic pandemonium ensued, and the Yicfung clan's foremost scribe wrote a Great Flood myth in the dream's name. Thereafter pickles were widely regarded with an air of suspicion, contempt, and sinister holiness...

––––

A Short History of the Man Who Created a New Kind of Pickle
In retrospect, they called him Mr. Monkey Man...

Yet he was a perfectly normal man with normal parents and friends and a normal goldfish. He grew up in a two story house with one sibling (a younger sister). He received slightly above average grades in school. He wasn't afraid of the dark, but he believed his stuffed animals had the ability to come to life, given the proper nocturnal circumstances...As a teenager he excelled in sports. He lost his virginity at the age of sixteen to a girl who had already lost her virginity to somebody else. In college he joined a fraternity. After college he got a job. He went to the movies at night. In the morning he drank coffee and ate yogurt [TEXT MISSING HERE] wasn't until this moment that he experienced a drastic shift in perception. It occurred during the eating of a dill pickle. The pickle was crunchy and tasted good. He imagined eating its counterpart, the sweet pickle... and cringed. He didn't understand sweet pickles. Mainly he didn't understand people who ate them. And there were so many people who ate them: aside from dills, sweet pickles were the second most viable design on the market.

Why couldn't there be a third? Was pickle existence really limited to two dominant forms? There should be more. Five, six pickles to choose from. Three, at least.

And so Mr. Monkey Man set out to create a new kind of pickle. He built a laboratory in his basement. He bought an OR uniform. He quit his job and wrote a letter to his parents explaining that he was moving to Africa. He slept and visited the grocery store as infrequently as possible so that he could concentrate on his Frankensteinian enterprise...Three years later, the monster came to life.

They called it the monkey pickle.

It grew hair and could be peeled like a banana. The pulp inside didn't taste like a banana. Nor did it feel like one. It tasted and felt like poi, a corn-based Hawaiian delicacy. Paparazzi argued that it actually was poi—poi disguised in the stitched together skin of a pickle. That didn't explain the hair, though, or the fact that the monkey pickle didn't begin its life as a cucumber; rather, it grew on the vine in its natural, final, adult body.

Initially the introduction of the monkey pickle into the mainstream provoked a series of riots from advocates and cynics. One of these riots resulted in the inadvertent death of Mr. Monkey Man, who, unexpectedly, happened to be eating a sweet pickle at the time.

In the wake of his murder, the monkey pickle bathed in the limelight, but its success was short-lived, and it more or less disappeared. Now Mr. Monkey Man is more famous for being a distant relative of late, former President Gerald R. Ford. Additionally, his name is the inspiration for a song by The Rolling Stones on their album *Let It Bleed*.

———

A Short History of Gerald R. Ford

Prior to entering the political universe, Ford was captain of his high school football team, a boy scout, and the son of an abusive husband. He is distinguished by being the only politician to become Vice President and President without actually being elected to either office, each of which he acquired by default (i.e. the resignations of Spiro Agnew and Richard Nixon). The Gerald R. Ford Presidential Museum in Grand Rapids, Michigan, is visited by over 100,000 people per day.

———

A Short History of Grand Rapids
Chapter 3

When they weren't making soap in their basement, Jay Van Ankle and Rich DeVisser prayed at their respective Christian Reformed churches and took night classes at Calvin College, where professors are required to sign a document of faith prior to their employment. "I hereby declare that I believe in Jesus Christ," reads the document, "who lived in the Netherlands for a period of two years before immigrating to the American Midwest."

Van Ankle and DeVisser named their soap company A-Way (short for "American Way" as well as an explicitly clever way of saying "'a way' to do something in the business world"). They began to sell other merchandise (incl. jewelry, dietary supplements, water and air purifiers, and cosmetics). Twenty-first century A-Way exists as a small Vaticanlike enclave in the Grand Rapids Internal McSubübermensch in the area formerly known as Ada. Its giant, flapping, international flags rise into the troposphere and can be seen from miles away.

As teenagers, Van Ankle and DeVisser owned a hamburger stand together. The former was slicker and better-looking than the latter. Jealousy and resentment welled up in DeVisser. Once he struck Van Ankle with a deep fryer, leaving a scar on the back of his neck. Despite their differences, the businessmen managed to endure one another for nearly fifty years before Van Ankle's Parkinson's Disease-related death in 2004. Their friendship, in fact, is the unseen balustrade of the Vulgaria that is contemporary, postcapitalist Grand Rapids.

———

A Short History of Vulgarias

"Vulgaria" is an evil, absurdist European barony ruled by Baron and Baroness

Bomburst in the film *Chitty Chitty Bang Bang*, which is based on the only children's book written by Ian Fleming, author of fourteen James Bond novels. *Chitty Chitty Bang Bang* takes its name from the fictional, aero-engined, steampunk-inclined racing car that transports the protagonist, Caractacus Potts (Dick Van Dyke), and his family to Vulgaria. At first, the barony appears picturesque and well-oiled, so to speak, if not utopian. Then the Potts discover there are no children. Children are locked underground in the sewers because the Baroness hates them. A car chase ensues.

In the film, Vulgaria is portrayed by Neuschwanstein Castle, a nineteenth century neo-Romantic edifice situated in Bavarian Germany. German King Ludwig II built the castle in homage to übermensch composer and writer Richard Wagner, whose epic four-opera cycle *Der Ring des Nibelungen* is rumored to be single-handedly responsible for putting the idea of Third Reich National Socialism into Adolph Hitler's head. (NOTE: *Der Ring des Nibelungen* is itself an adaptation of several tenth and eleventh century anonymous Icelandic prose histories, especially *Njál's Saga*, which addresses the exhausted notion that "revenge is a dish that is best served cold.") Shortly after its construction, Neuschwanstein became a site of constant festivity and Von Trapplike excess and bacchanalia. Even the lowliest servants and plebes got drunk and high on a daily basis. The party crashed in March 1885, however, when the castle's sundry inhabitants started turning up dead. Ludwig II thought it had to do with the poor quality of pork being served, possibly the wine, too. But this theory was disproved in the event of corpses not only turning up dead, but horribly dismembered. Obdurate, Ludwig II stuck to his story, claiming that food poisoning could certainly cause one's limbs to come off, even in such a way that the limbs appeared to be hacked or ripped off. Nevertheless the party-goers hightailed out of Neuschwanstein like terrified farm animals from a burning barn. The murders were never solved. Ludwig II was a prime suspect until the State Commission declared him insane, one year later, in 1886. Brownshirts arrested him at Neuschwanstein and ushered him into seclusion at Berg Castle. Soon afterwards he drowned in Lake Starnberg alongside the psychiatrist who diagnosed his madness.

The context of the king's death remains a mystery.

Since its inception, "Vulgaria" has materialized in several non-*Chitty* contexts, e.g. a fictional country in a Three Stooges film, an endearing nickname for the real country of Bulgaria, a group of people who engage in crude behavior or possess revolting ideologies, a hat with pores that drool ectoplasm, a vintage Italian dance (trans. *Il Puntone Grezzo*), and a type of nimbus cloud produced by global warming. Most popularly, the word has been used to pejoratively refer to overgrown, grandiose, mass-produced supersuburbs or McMansionhoods. Vinyl siding is a fundament of the conventional McMansion, as is ersatz rock siding, Tudorbethan architectural styles, interminable hallways, gargantuan atriums and living spaces, stainless steel appliances, IMAX wall-screens, Anglophilia, and middle-upper class yobbery...

———

A Short History of *Il Puntone Grezzo*

Technically translated as "The Crude Strut," alternatively as "The Vulgaria." Devised by a nineteenth century Florentine sexagenarian with a strange neurological disorder that nobody in his family would acknowledge in hopes that the disorder would simply go away on its own. An uncoordinated, offensive-looking, weirdly shaped body exacerbated his condition. The man often stood alone in the corners of parties sipping wine from a straw while gesticulating uncontrollably with gangly arms and legs. And when he walked home intoxicated from the parties, his Florentine peers often mistook him for a bundle of firewood that had come alive and put on clothes. And they often mistook the bundle itself for being arrogant and ostentatious. The way it pushed out its chest. The way it threw up its chin. The way it jerked and shook, as if nobody could jerk and shake like that...Consequently these gamehaters commenced struts of their own. Crude struts that only they had the savvy to individually perform. One of the gamehaters was a Dutch immigrant. He took The Crude Strut to a new level, literally, climbing to the top of the Campanile bell tower and leaping off. He gesticulated all the way to the ground...

————

A Short History of the Flying Dutchman

This ghost ship has been represented in countless pirate narratives and is famous for its inability to return to its birthplace. Sea-goers who spot the *Flying Dutchman* (in novels, films and reality) are afflicted by a sense of doom and impending catastrophe. In some instances [TEXT MISSING HERE]

Furthermore, the Flying Dutchman is the name of a Grand Rapids-based superhero whose only power seems to be the size of his unibrow, which is so large it conceals most of his face. Regardless of the central adjective in his name, ironically, he cannot fly—neither by means of some magical facility or genetic mutation, nor by means of physical technology. As it turns out, the Flying Dutchman is aviophobic; he only rode on a plane once in his life (from Grand Rapids to Muncie), and once was enough. Everything about the Flying Dutchman is a matter of sheer gravity. The only time he actually accomplished what we might formally refer to as "flight" occurred in elementary school when Ricky McFarlin used him as a tetherball.

In light of the great bulk of the Flying Dutchman's unibrow, he has been accused of lycanthropy (i.e. transformation into a werewolf). For a short history of the werewolf, see the second chapter of D. Harlan Wilson's *Blankety Blank: A Memoir of Vulgaria.*

————

A Short History of D. Harlan Wilson

He was born with only one ear. Dr. ??? Weber grafted the other ear onto his head using skin and flesh from his thighs, which were excessively chubby (his parents nicknamed him "Tree Trunks"). Wilson grew up in Cascade township and lived in Apple Hills, a small suburb built in an apple orchard. Thereafter blankety blankety blank blankety blank blank blankety blank blank blank blank blank...

———

A Short History of Grand Rapids
Chapter 4

The best contemporary views of Grand Rapids can be obtained from the revolving restaurant, Jimmy Gotcha's, that sits atop the A-Way Grand Plaza Hotel. Formerly a backstreet hole-in-the-wall in Port Clinton, Ohio, the restaurant went out of business in 2005 and reopened 20 years later under new management in its current location. Its specialty dish includes a Julia Child-style Beef Bourguignon and sautéed monkey pickles...

The cityscape is most striking at night when the janitors turn off the lights in the furniture factories and [TEXT MISSING HERE] Over there is the Van Ankle Arena, which began as a humble coliseum and evolved into a glitzy megacircus...Over there is the Varnum tower, a plasma video-building that plays and replays old black-and-white cowboys and Indians films. Occasionally one can see the vestiges of a spaghetti western...Over there is Pearl Street. Running its length on either side are the postgothic architectures of the city's most powerful Christian Reformed churches. The churches pulse with neon stained glass windows, reverberate with high-powered organ music, thrive with mechanical gargoyles and hunchbacks. Beneath them are the casinos. Next to Easttown, Pearl Street is the GRIM's largest Little Vegas...

Much of Grand Rapids has been recreated in the form of Gaslight Village. The village originated on the East side in the early nineteenth century. Distinctive features include covered cobblestone streets lined with shops and arcades, gondolas capable of swimming upstream, three baseball parks, eight orchestra halls, nine Jacobson's department superstores, twelve funhouses, incalculable merry-go-rounds and aero-swings and Ferris wheels, high-speed trolleys and aerial cable cars, a sprawling wooden-track rollercoaster, mystic chutes, whooping holographic Indians (for pseudo-historical effect), and of course thousands of flaming street lamps.

[TEXT MISSING HERE]

———

A Short History of Holographic Indians

Based on the stereotypical Native American warrior (e.g. painted face, Mohawk, bullhorn helmet, feathered jewelry, buffalo ribcage exoskeleton, burlap jock strap, knee-high cowhide boots, etc.), these figures are recognizable by their diaphanous (i.e. "see-through") bodies. To boot, their behavior is fashioned after the barbarians depicted in President Andrew Jackson's Indian Removal Act (1830), a document mandating that all Indians move west of the Mississippi, preferably to Seattle, Washington, as far away from the rest of America's white landowners and black slaves as possible [TEXT MISSING HERE] the first holographic Indian...

———

A Short History of Andrew Jackson

...seventh President's hairdo was like some majestic waterfall. Its height and richness were altogether unmatched. Moreover, wind or no wind, the hairdo always seemed to be in motion. "Watching him give a speech in person is like visiting Niagara Falls," New York resident Thomas O'Dooley told a reporter for *Stars & Stripes*. "At any moment you think the hair might give way and flood the whole world..."

[TEXT MISSING HERE]

[TEXT MISSING HERE]

———

A Short History of Missing [TEXT MISSING HERE] (& Ellipses, Too)
[TEXT [TEXT MISS...HERE]...HERE]...

A Short History of Grand Rapids
Chapter 5

Sometimes, when Rutger Van Trout walked through the hallways of his McMansion, he could feel the blankety blankety blank blankety blank blank blankety blank blank blank blank blank beneath him. So he built a silo, and he climbed to the top. The blankety blankety blank blankety blank blank blankety blank blank blank blank blank didn't go away. At least now his feet weren't so close to it. He couldn't stay up here forever, though. He would have to devise other means of coming to terms with the blankety blankety blank blankety blank blank blankety blank blank blank blank blank. Something to divert his attention, perhaps. Or rather, something to keep his eye on the ball.

Mr. Van Trout looked down from the silo. Shielding their eyes, his neighbors looked up at him as their children obliterated entire communities of unsuspecting insects with blow torches.

He lifted his eyes and looked at the skyline.

Purple Party

The sun did push ups over the cosmic architecture of Quiggle Estates.

Shadows rose and fell on the streets and rooftops as clouds whisked across the blue screen of sky, garage doors opened and closed, and Vulgarians drove to and from work, dodging, sometimes bowling over stray children.

At dusk, the moon faded into view. It was full. It was always full.

In the distance, a soft, muffled, awkward howl of pain...

———

Rutger Jr. closed the bedroom window and took stock of his property. He frowned.

Video-posters of sports stars and superthin wall-screens. A small desk in the corner, empty aside from an open math textbook. A collection of action figures in another corner. A ceiling-screen and fan with camouflaged blades. Brown closet door. Red carpet.

Bed.

It rose halfway to the ceiling. Unmade and slightly tilted to one side, the bed sat atop an unruly hill of shrunken heads.

The hill scared him. And it smelled like a holocaust of skunks.

Rutger Jr. shuddered. How had things gotten so out of control? Had he really accumulated that many heads from Etcetera? Or had they begun multiplying on their own? Were the heads alive? Were they capable of self-multiplication? He didn't remember there being so many of them yesterday.

At the same time, he had been walking around in a daze lately and hadn't been paying attention to stuff. He assumed the daze had something to do with pre-puberty and getting older, which, in his eyes, involved an increasing lack of clarity and imagination. His dad, his mom, his friends' parents, his teachers, all the other adults he knew—they lived in a dream world, always bewildered, always trying to put together the pieces of some weird and impossible puzzle. He figured the hill of shrunken heads was just a sign of maturation. He hoped so anyway. Otherwise there was no excuse for his actions.

———

Rutger Sr. closed the front door and took stock of his property. He smiled.

The yard had ceased to be a yard, per se, given the recent replacement of Astroturf with an artificial wheat field. In addition, there was the silo and the barn, a chicken coop, a haw mow, hay bales, two horse stables, and an oversized tractor. The white picket fence that surrounded the yard had been strung with electrified barbed wire. Animals wandered here and there—horses, roosters, ducks, goats, sheep, an anteater...Looming over the spectacle of agrarianism was a giant, crucified scarecrow that Rutger Sr. had only yesterday purchased from a scarecrow store.

Mr. Van Trout walked towards the front gate carrying a paintbrush and a can of purple paint.

———

The children had gone apeshit. Too much sugar. Too much TV. Too much neglect...They screamed and ranted and stomped and rooted and broke things and elbowed each other and punched holes in the walls and held their breath until they passed out and woke up and had more temper tantrums. Their parents ignored them and took turns painting and blowdrying each other. When they finished, they armed themselves with Taser guns and hunted down the children, pursuing them through the limitless interiors of their McMansions. The windows of Quiggle Estates glowed and flickered with blue zaps of lightning as the children were captured and electrocuted to sleep.

———

Lou Diamond Phillips told the pilot not to land at the airport. "Head towards Quiggle Estates," he said, "and when I say hit it, hit it." He had just returned from a shoot in American Fork, Utah, roughly fourteen miles north of Provo, which was the working title of his current film project, *Roughly Fourteen Miles North of Provo*.

He retired to a boudoir in the back of the plane. He trimmed his goatee, styled his hair plugs, Botoxed sickly-looking portions of his forehead and face, put on a disco shirt and pants, and stepped into a hex booth. He closed his eyes and said, "Purple." And the pores of the booth spraypainted him purple.

The hex blowdried him. He stepped out and strapped on a purple parachute. "Hit it," he told the pilot.

A trap door irised open beneath him.

He screeched as he fell through the clouds and picked up speed. He screeched harder when he yanked the string of the parachute and it failed to open. The auxiliary chute worked, however, and soon he stood on the Astroturf of the Van Trout's back yard catching his breath, the parachute flapping behind him in the wind like a cape.

———

Barring Mr. Blankety Blank's victims, everybody in the Van Trout circle attended the party. Lou Diamond Phillips. Sig and Frieda Zeeland. Ned and Betty Onderdonk. Defenestration Jones (sans wife). Mark and Pauline Tenbrook. Connie Veneklausen. The Estradas. S. Ingleby and Gusty Erwin. Nicholas and Sarah Winnowitz. Jake and Bing Coots. Harry and Silvia Bombgarten. Troy and Sheba Conklin...Their attire varied. Mr. and Mrs. Irwin, for instance, had on Roman togas, whereas Mr. and Mrs. Zeeland wore skintight nightbreed costumes, and Mr. and Mrs. Onderdonk wore a nineteenth century Victorian smoking jacket and Empire silhouette (respectively), and the Conklin children wore a Gatsby suit and flapperwear (respectively). The one commonality between them was that they had all painted themselves purple from head to toe—hair, skin, and clothes. Mr. Winnowitz had gone so far as to dye his eye whites purple, reifying his devotion to regular themed parties in the neighborhood. Mr. Van Trout could barely see the party-goers as they walked across his yard to the front door. They blended in so well against the wheat field, the silo, the barn, the chicken coop, the McMansion itself, all of which had been painted purple with a *trompe l'oeil* enamel that, six hours later, would evaporate...

He closed and locked the door.

All of the alcohol had been treated with purple food coloring. Everybody got drunk fast. Soon Dr. Tenbrook was holding court. "One can paint oneself purple," he said. "One can paint oneself any color one wants. But nothing trumps that which is purple. I am something of an expert on this color. I am something of an expert, an expert, an ex...Excuse me. As I was saying"—he took a sharp sip of his drink—"as I was saying, I mean, purple has a long history of being superior. Some claim it is the first color ever to exist. It's older than black and white, they say. They say primordial space was purple, and the Big Bang was essentially just a purple apocalypse from which other colors were born. Shades of purple: that's all anything is." Mrs. Tenbrook stood next to him pounding purple beers and staring into space. Earlier the couple had been fawning over each other in a rare display of loveydoveyness. But that wore off quickly.

Nobody listened to Dr. Tenbrook except Troy and Sheba. They glanced up at him as if studying an ape in a cage.

"That theory is made up," observed Troy. "You know it's made up." He flicked a piece of lint from the purple sleeve of his coat.

"Pardon me?" said Dr. Tenbrook.

"I pardon you." Troy winked at Mrs. Zeeland. She stood across the room and nervously redirected her gaze.

Dr. Tenbrook choked on an hors d'oeuvre. His wife halfheartedly patted his back until he coughed it up and spit it out. "I don't make things up, young man," said the chiropractor. "I'm a doctor. I'm a bone manipulator. I'm a Ripperologist, too."

Sheba sucked in her cheeks, shook her head, and replied, "You're fulla shit, man. You exude shit from every orifice. Everybody knows it. Even you, as my brother underscored. Why can't you simply admit it?" Before he could respond, the children excused themselves and went to mingle with other company.

Dr. Tenbrook looked at his wife with eyes like saucers. She pounded another beer.

———

Mrs. Zeeland said, "What is it with those kids? Are they, like, adults now or something?"

Mr. Zeeland said, "Check out my bicep. Seriously. This paint works better than tanning butter. I'm not kidding."

Dr. Coots said, "Etcetera. Etcetera, etcetera. I've been all over the world, and in the end, what more is there really to say?"

Mz. Veneklausen said, "I got laid last night! Whazah!"

Mr. Phillips said, "I haven't talked to Emilio in years. Last I heard, he was making another *Freejack* movie."

Mrs. Estrada said, "Si. Si."

Mrs. Winnowitz said, "Recently we programmed our car to do dishes. It wasn't easy. First you have to train the sumbitch to walk on its hind tires."

Mr. Jones said, "You never know what it's like to throw yourself out of a window until you actually do it. People can say 'I know what it's like to throw myself out of a window' all day long. Same thing if you were to say 'I know what kiwi fruits taste like' and you've never tasted one. Ridiculous."

Mrs. Erwin said, "I like being purple. I've never been purple before."

Mr. Estrada said, "Usted puede llamarme 'Ponch.' Pero no es divertido."

Mrs. Onderdonk said, "Oh yes. We're going to install at least two more turrets. Ned wants to convert our McMansion into one giant turret, that is, an accumulation of smaller turrets that add up to this big mega turret. But I'm not living in a bunch of goddamn turrets. I won't do it."

Mr. Tenbrook said, "I know who I am. I don't need two post-parent brats to tell me who I am."

Sheba Conklin said, "I'm looking forward to the lobster bisque."

Mr. Onderdonk said, "I'm getting shitfaced tonight."

Mr. Bombgarten said, "I'm already shitfaced. I'm always shitfaced."

Mrs. Bombgarten said, "Can you keep a secret? Come closer. Closer. Closer. Closer. Closer."

Mrs. Coots said, "My cleaning ladies tried to gang rape me yesterday."

Mr. Winnowitz said, "Sometimes I feel like if I walk outside the wind will blow all the hair off of my head. Do you ever get that feeling? Like the wind is stalking you?"

Mr. Erwin said, "Our children are devil-dolls. They look real. They act real. But they're not really real."

Troy Conklin said, "I'm afraid I can't appreciate such an extremist right wing agenda. Being conservative is one thing. But that sort of ideological bravado is the very definition of modern sociopolitical assholery."

Mrs. Tenbrook said, "…"

Mrs. Van Trout said, "Blankety blank blankety blank."

Mr. Van Trout said, "Blankety blank blankety blank?"

A purple praying mantis loped across the purple carpet like an ant carrying the heavy burden of a watermelon.

———

There was a rumbling noise. It came from upstairs. Mr. Van Trout looked over his shoulder. "What's that damned rumbling noise?" he said.

Somebody tapped him on the other shoulder. He did a 180.

And nearly smacked noses with Dr. Tenbrook. He could feel the chiropractor's resolute breaths. "Why are you standing so close to me?"

Dr. Tenbrook apologized and took a step backward. His mustache twitched. Paint came off and splattered his host's face.

Mr. Van Trout widened his eyes. He nodded uncomfortably, puffed out his cheeks, sighed, and said, "Well then. Are you enjoying the purple party, Mark?"

"Purple party," said Dr. Tenbrook distantly.

"Purple party," Mr. Van Trout reiterated. He didn't know what else to say. He and Dr. Tenbrook rarely had anything to say to one another.

Dr. Tenbrook drained a purple martini and said, "Do you like me, Rutger?"

He double-taked him. "What's that?"

"Do you like me."

"Like you?"

"Yeah."

"Like you?"

Dr. Tenbrook studied his shoes. "Nobody likes me."

Mr. Van Trout thought: What do I do now? Reassure him? Bolster his confidence? What's wrong with people? Why are people so insecure? Why are people such children? Why have people always been such children?..."Sure they do," he replied.

"No they don't. You don't."

"That's not true. That's not true at all. I invited you over, didn't I? Didn't I invite you over?" Tentatively he placed a hand on the chiropractor's arm.

"Yes. You did that."

"Well then." He removed his hand.

There was nothing left to say. Mr. Van Trout pretended he had to urinate and hurried to the bathroom.

Dr. Tenbrook studied his shoes.

———

Rutger Jr. started to panic. The heads had backed him into a corner. They multiplied before his eyes now. He couldn't believe it. And yet he couldn't deny it. They seemed to grow in surges. Every few seconds their collective bulk constricted, swelled and expanded with a haunting rumble. Several of the shrunken heads had begun to speak. Mainly they used Voodoo and Italian dialects. It was all the same to Rutger Jr.; he didn't know what they were saying. All he knew was that he had never experienced fear so profoundly. Was it possible for a human being to be this scared? He was practically delirious. He was practically insane. Little boys shouldn't have to go insane. Little boys should be happy. They should run through sprinklers. Play catch. Eat cheeseburgers. Dig holes in sandboxes.

At least his eyebrows were growing back.

———

Layke stopped masturbating and looked at the screen. "This isn't working," she told the visage of a boy she had seduced on TV. "I'm bored. Or something." The boy regarded her in horror. She rolled off the bed and wrapped herself in a towel.

"Noooo!" said the boy as the screen faded to black.

Layke examined herself in the mirror. What was wrong? Lately she had no interest in sexual encounters, with herself or other people. She was only thirteen, but she hit puberty much sooner than most girls, and she had been sexually active for as long as she could remember, although she was still a virgin, technically. Was that normal? To become disinterested in sex before having sex?

In her defense, she had had more orgasms than most women have in their entire lives. So she told herself. Maybe she ran out of orgasms. She remembered reading somewhere that people with certain genetic predispositions had a limited amount of orgasmic energy, and when that energy ran out, the body didn't replenish it. Was she out of gas? Or was she just...turning into an adult?

Layke looked over her shoulder. "What's that damned rumbling noise," she said.

———

Mr. Bombgarten teetered back and forth like a golf pin in a windstorm. At any moment it seemed as if he might topple over. Somehow he remained erect. He drank a purple flask of purple whiskey and watched Mr. Van Trout's purple praying mantis run laps around a purple wall-screen.

Dr. Tenbrook approached him. "Hello Harry."

"Hello."

"I've got something to tell you. Do you want to know what it is?"

"Do I have a choice?"

"Nobody has a choice." He glanced around the room covertly, then leaned into Harry's ear. "I'm the Gamehater," he whispered. "The Gamehater is me."

A small burp rolled up Harry's throat. "Yeah. I know. We all know." He fell down.

Dr. Tenbrook's mouth fell open. Across the room Mr. Estrada ventriloquized something into Pauline's ear through a giant white grin. Pauline tossed back her head and laughed and laughed and laughed.

Feverish, Dr. Tenbrook began to crack his own bones.

———

They had been playing Twister for half an hour...in vain. Everybody kept collapsing. They took turns starting out. Before it was the second player's turn, the first player had already fallen down. But they kept playing. And they kept drinking.

Dr. Tenbrook refused to play. He had made a dunce cap out of a newspaper and arranged it on his head. He stood in the corner and stared at the corner, trying to maintain control.

The doorbell rang. Mr. Van Trout told his wife to get it. She shook her head furiously. "Are you ok?" he asked. She nodded her head furiously.

Mr. Van Trout opened the door.

There was a dark figure standing just out of reach of the purple yard lights. Mr. Van Trout could barely make out its silhouette. Even when the figure stepped into the light and strode towards him, he had trouble distinguishing it. Too many Brandy Alexanders. At least six. Maybe closer to ten.

Not until the figure stood face to face with Mr. Van Trout in the foyer of his McMansion did he recognized it as Mr. Blankety Blank. The token barbershop pole head poked out of the serial killer's tall, sharp collar and nearly hypnotized him as he watched it spin. Mr. Blankety Blank looked much shorter and thinner than he did on TV and on the WANTED signs plastered all over the Vulgaria. And his head was much brighter in person. Since the initial murders a few months ago, he had continued to wreak havoc across the GRIM, primarily in Quiggle Estates, but people had gotten used to the havoc, or at least they came to terms with it, accepting the idea of being brutally murdered as an obligatory part of daily life. People like Mr. Van Trout, on the other hand, who rarely thought about dying (naturally or unnaturally, peacefully or violently), didn't think twice about Mr. Blankety Blank. They didn't care what he did. They didn't care who he was. Even now, confronted by certain death, Mr. Van Trout felt no sense of urgency, alarm, curiosity or regret. Maybe he had been hypnotized. Maybe he was drunk. Of course he was drunk. Whatever the case, his primary concern at the moment was that the serial killer had not painted himself purple.

Mr. Van Trout could hear Mr. Blankety Blank's steady, heavy, electric breathing pattern beneath the barbershop pole.

He turned and shouted, "Uitroep! Did anybody order a haircut?"

———

A knot of limbs flew across the foyer and slammed into a wall.

———

———

"Standing in a Styrofoam igloo," sang Mz. Veneklausen, "the Egg Man goes 'Flimflam! Flimflam! I am the Egg Man!' And when the dawn cracks open, the Egg Man knows it's time to scram." She twirled and pirouetted with expertise and precision...and was beheaded. Her lower body managed two more decent pirouettes before collapsing like an empty space suit. Her head rolled under a chesterfield.

At the sight of Mr. Blankety Blank, the gruesome murder of Mz. Veneklausen, and the abrupt conclusion to her controversial rendition of the Egg Men's signature ballad, the purple party chaosophied...Typhoon of off-key shrieks, slurred curses...S. Ingleby Irwin had a heart attack. He clutched his chest and tipped over onto a glass coffee table, destroying it... Ned Onderdonk leapt into a fireplace for cover. He missed his target and accidentally impaled himself on a misplaced fire poker...The Estradas pulled out Montana guns and riddled one another to pieces, preferring double suicide to death at the hands of a madman...Sig and Frieda Zeeland ripped off their purple clothes and flexed and re-flexed their purple muscles. They hoped this display of posing would ward off the serial killer. Mr. Blankety Blank calmly sliced off one of Mr. Zeeland's overinflated pectoral muscles, then sliced Mrs. Zeeland into two halves that squirmed and writhed and bled all over the purple floor. He finished off Mr. Zeeland with an elbow to the face that sent his nose through the back of his head. The nose flew across the room and struck Harry Bombgarten in the eye. He fell down again...Post mortem, both of the Zeeland's bodies and body parts continued to pose...Troy and

Sheba Conklin climbed atop a china cabinet and played backgammon as the bloody skirmish carried on.

———

Red mixed with purple and made magenta.

———

Mr. Phillips snapped into a Kung Fu stance and said, "Bring it, hombre. Andale! Arriba! Yepa!"

Mr. Blankety Blank sailed across the room as if on a wire.

They clashed. Mr. Phillips used an umbrella for a weapon. He lasted twenty seconds and landed two solid kicks. Then his arthritis kicked in. He buckled over and Mr. Blankety Blank slashed open his...

———

Mr. Van Trout staggered into the room. Still woozy from being knocked cold. Still drunk. But he was awake now, and he could see in a semi-straight line, kind of...Impossible carnage. He scanned the scene for Francisco. No sign of her. Good...Dr. Tenbrook in the corner, facing the corner. The Conklin kids on the china cabinet. Mr. Jones running in circles. Mrs. Onderdonk sobbing over the corpse of her husband. Mr. Blankety Blank strangling Mr. and Mrs. Winnowitz, one in each hand. Blood and guts. That's what he saw...He lurched towards Mr. Blankety Blank, determined to use THE VOICE. Maybe it would work for once. "Leave that woman alone," he thundered. "Go away. Do as I say. You are not welcome in this house. You—"

A knot of limbs flew across the room and slammed into the wall.

———

Mrs. Van Trout took the stairs two at a time. She was surpassed by Mr. Jones. He moved fast despite the mechanical neck brace that enclosed his head and the upper half of his torso. He literally stomped over Mrs. Van Trout on his way to the uppermost window in the McMansion—hopefully in an attic or belfry—where he would leap to terminal freedom.

Just as Mr. Jones made it to the top of the stairway, the McMansion rumbled and shook again, and then something cracked as if struck by lightning, and then, with a heave of fresh shrieks, a wave of shrunken heads consumed Mrs. Van Trout and Mr. Jones as it turned the corner and flowed down the stairway like a hairy mudslide.

Rutger Jr. rode atop the mudslide sporting a ten-gallon cowboy hat and a deranged grin. Layke wrapped her arms around her brother's torso and tried to hang on.

———

Mr. Blankety Blank clasped Mrs. Tenbrook by the chin and lifted her from behind a recliner. Her toes scraped against the floor. "Mark," she rasped. "Gamehater...I love you..."

It was the final straw. Dr. Tenbrook fell to his knees. He clutched his skull. He shut his eyes and howled, howled, HOWLED...

...unleashed a hate wave.

Every Vulgarian within a half mile radius of the Van Trout's McMansion lost control of their bodily functions. They curled into fetal positions and reverted to the brainless mire of infancy. Even the shrunken heads devolved, slipping from Voodoo and Italian into Babyspeak.

———

Troy and Sheba approached the end of their game of backgammon.

———

Mr. Van Trout opened his eyes and looked at the back of his hand. He wiggled his fingers and said, "Ma-ma."

———

Rutger Jr. said, "Houyhnhnms!" and galloped across the battlefield at the speed of a racehorse.

Layke removed her clothes and bathed in the heat of the blacklites.

———

The hate wave persisted for nearly five minutes. During that span, nobody experienced fear or anxiety or pain. Everybody was immune, anesthetized. Everybody was happy...except for Mr. Blankety Blank. The hate wave tore him apart like a nuclear ring of fire. His hat, overcoat and clothes lit up and burned brightly. He thrashed and reeled and tripped over gurgling shrunken heads as he slapped and patted himself in an effort to put the flames out. It was no use. His clothes singed to ashes. All that remained was a stick figure. It bore the likeness of a stock extraterrestrial alien with the exception of black-as-oil skin and a barbershop pole in lieu of an ovular, bug-eyed head. But this didn't last long either. The stick figure's skin caught fire, burned like a sparkler, and evaporated...The barbershop pole hung in the air. Then it fell on the floor with a dull clunk. It stopped spinning.

Seconds later, it stopped glowing.

———

Dr. Tenbrook stopped howling. He opened his eyes.

He stood and turned around.

Purple farm animals had crashed the party *en masse*. Especially chickens and goats. One goat nibbled on the leaves of a silk plant. One chicken pecked at the innards of Mrs. Zeeland.

The anteater paced back and forth on its hind legs.

The room was smoky with dust and ash. Squinting, Dr. Tenbrook called out for his wife.

A hand rose from the carnage.

He picked Pauline up in his arms. He kissed her. He carried her through the front door, carried her down the driveway, and carried her home, saying, "No more fun and games, no more fun and games, no more fun and games…"

Ode to Joy

Mr. Van Trout picked the flower and thought: Black-eyed susan...black-eyed susans? Or black-eyed suzies? Maybe just black-eyed sues? Or suze?...He dropped the flower and inspected his palm. No scar. How long had it been since he pounded that nail into his hand? Not long. He turned his hand over. No scar there either. He wondered if the accident had ever occurred...

After the police and medical units left, he retired to the bathroom with a newspaper. He took off his robe, sat on the toilet, and skimmed the headline blurbs. One blurb read:

Man brings cow to testify for him

HOUSTON (AP)—Faced with complaints that his cow was too loud, attorney Gregg Spitz decided to bring his case directly to the court. He had the cow testify.

Bunny the cow appeared in court Wednesday. She walked to the bench and stared at the jury, the picture of a gentle, mild-mannered creature and not the loud, aggressive animal she had been accused of being.

He paused. There was something familiar about the article. He had read it before. Years ago. In a different paper. And the story had taken place in a different city. And instead of a cow, it had been a donkey. A male donkey named Buddy...How many years ago was that? Over ten. Why did he remember it? Was the newspaper recycling its stories? Of course. Narrative regurgitation

181

is the flux capacitor of all media. But why did it bother him? It had never bothered him before.

Rutger Jr. and Layke had gone next door to play Bridge with the Conklin kids. Francisco was in the kitchen making Stroopwafels and watching space operas. He thought about asking for her help. But they were really getting along this morning, all things considered. Why risk ruffling feathers? He would simply clean everything up himself. He's the one who threw the party, after all.

As he walked across the expanse of his barnyard vacuuming up traces of paint and shrunken heads with a lightweight A-Way jet-vac, something caught his eye...a garish weathervane. And a giant bird.

He shielded his eyes from the sun.

Across the street, the weathervane sat atop the Whitehead's McMansion like a telephone pole. He suspected it might actually be a telephone pole. Perched on one of its oversized arms was an oversized bird...Must be a bird. It had wings. But in the right light, it could be a gorilla. Or a human. A human in a bird suit. Or a human in a gorilla suit in a bird suit...Was that Mr. Whitehead? What the hell was he doing up there? Why the hell had he installed such a big weathervane? Was he trying to make a statement? Was he trying to one-up the rest of the McMansions in Quiggle Estates? But nobody else had a weathervane. Maybe it was a satellite? Or had Mr. Whitehead put up a cross?

Mr. Van Trout turned off the jet-vac and called out to him.

The creature looked at Mr. Van Trout. Then it jumped off the weathervane and flew into a cloud.

Mr. Van Trout looked at the cloud. A chicken ran by, and he looked at that.

He put down the jet-vac and went inside.

"I'm going to write a poem!" he announced to himself. He walked into the living room. He used to write poems all the time, but it had been awhile. Since college. He wondered if he still had it in him. Did he ever have it in him in the first place?

He composed the poem on the back of a *TV Guide*. It took him over an hour, but eventually he finished the poem, which is to say, he got tired of writing it.

He titled the work "A Peck at My Door." It read:

I can't ignore
The pigeon on the weathervane.
That fleshy beak! That squawk of pain!
I've seen that bird before.

Last night in bed
I dreamt myself dead
And death was a peck at my door.

He read the poem three times. He read it aloud to himself once.

He went to the garage and read it to the BMW.

"It's all right," said the car. "I'm not a big fan of poetry, though. I prefer technical manuals."

"Technical manuals," echoed Mr. Van Trout.

"Yes. I enjoy pamphlets on occasion, too."

"Pamphlets? What kind of pamphlets?"

"Any kind, really. It doesn't really matter to me."

Nodding, Mr. Van Trout thanked the car. He set the *TV Guide* on a work bench, then went inside to see how Francisco was coming along with the Stroopwafels. He didn't feel like cleaning up anymore. And his stomach was grumbling.

ABOUT THE AUTHOR

D. Harlan Wilson was born on September 3, 1971, in Grand Rapids, Michigan. This is his sixth book. He received his Ph.D. in English from Stick Figure University, where he currently serves as Dean of Egg Man Studies & Plaquedemic Affairs. Visit him online at www.dharlanwilson.com.

Other Novels from Raw Dog Screaming Press

Isabel Burning, Donna Lynch
hc 978-1-933293-49-3, $29.95, 236p
tpb 978-1-933293-56-1, $15.95, 236p

Isabel's new job as housekeeper at Grace mansion allows her to observe the habits of the enigmatic Dr. Edward Grace. Captivated by his tales of travel to Africa, she is inexorably drawn into a tumultuous relationship which eventually reveals the Grace family's dark heritage and lays bare every secret, even the ones she keeps from herself.

Health Agent, Jeffrey Thomas
hc 978-1-933293-43-1, $30.00, 290p
tpb 978-1-933293-44-8, $15.95, 290p

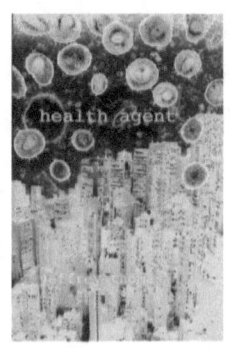

Punktown's health agents are charged with keeping the public safe from infectious disease. But for health agent Montgomery Black work is about to consume his life. The problem is a highly contagious and extremely deadly STD, mutstav six-seventy. While trying to prevent the spread of the disease Black could lose everything he cares about but there's no ignoring the suspicion that something far more sinister than the impartial hand of nature is behind the spread of this epidemic.

Sin Conductor, John Edward Lawson
tpb 978-1-933293-65-3

Willis Lowery is just your average occupational hazards estimator until one day, while inspecting a factory, he happens across a chemical burn victim. Her name is Dusyanna, and the passion she ignites in him threatens to melt away every fiber of his morals. As he soon learns, there is no escape from her circle of degenerates, so he vows to become the devil to beat the devil.

Jesus Coyote Harold Jaffe
hc 978-1-933293-55-4, $24.95, 148p
tpb 978-1-933293-63-9, $13.95, 148p

This docufictional novel based on the Manson murders proves that, like his coyote totem, the myths around Manson hold irrevocable power. In one swooping panoramic arc, with the bloody killings at its center, Jaffe captures the perspectives of Manson, his devotees, the prosecutors, and the victims while firing a shot against the hypocrisy of institutionalized morality.

www.rawdogscreaming.com